Susan Hawthorne writes fiction, poetry and non-fiction. A novel, *The Falling Woman* was published in 1992, and in 1993 her collection of poems, *The Language in my Tongue* was published in the volume *Four New Poets*. Her fiction, poetry and non-fiction have been published in magazines and anthologies in Australia, New Zealand, Europe and North America, and a German translation of *The Spinifex Quiz Book* will be published in 1994. In 1989 she received the Pandora Florence James Award for Outstanding Contribution to Women's Publishing.

Other books by Susan Hawthorne:

Anthologies
Difference (1985)
Moments of Desire (1989/90) with Jenny Pausacker
The Exploding Frangipani (1990) with Cathie Dunsford
Angels of Power (1991) with Renate Klein

Poetry
The Language in My Tongue/Four New Poets (1993)

Spinifex is an Australian native desert grass that is drought resistant and holds the earth together. In central Australia spinifex grass is traditionally burnt by Aboriginal people as a means of regenerating the land.

The Spinifex Quiz Book

A Book of Women's

~ • Answers • ~

SUSAN HAWTHORNE

SPINIFEX

Spinifex Press Pty Ltd,
504 Queensberry Street,
North Melbourne, Vic. 3051
Australia

First published by Spinifex Press, 1991
Second edition published 1993

Typeset in Garamond Light by Claire Warren, Melbourne
Made and Printed in Australia by The Book Printer, Victoria

National Library of Australia
Cataloguing-in-Publication entry:
CIP
Hawthorne, Susan, 1951–
 The Spinifex quiz book.

 2nd ed.
 Bibliography.
 Includes index.
 ISBN 1 875559 15 9.

1. Women – Miscellanea. I. Hawthorne, Susan, 1951–   . Spinifex
book of women's answers. II. Title. III. Title: Spinifex book of
women's answers.

305.42

Contents

Acknowledgements

There are many women to thank for both the genesis and the final shape of this book. The idea for the book came up in a meeting of the Australian Feminist Book Fortnight group, because there was a genuinely collective need for such a book. My thanks to the group for the idea. Thanks, too, to the individuals in the group who provided the initial questions: Judith Rodriguez, Sue Martin, Kate Veitch and, in particular, Jennifer Lang who provided numerous questions and organized them into sections. I would also like to thank Cathie Dunsford, Diana Ellerton, Sandy Jeffs, Renate Klein, Jocelynne Scutt, Dale Spender and Lynne Spender for providing questions in areas I knew little about and which helped the overall balance of the book. I would like to acknowledge the writers of the books in the bibliography, as well as other books not listed, without whose research this book would simply not have been possible. Finally, thanks to the magical workings of Claire Warren, typesetter extraordinaire, to Elizabeth Wood Ellem for her fantastic index, and to Liz Nicholson for her imaginative cover design.

Introduction

Did you know that the first known writer in the world was a woman; as was the first novelist? But it is not only in areas such as writing that women are responsible for cultural advancement. Many cultures credit a female deity with creating the world and with inventing all manner of things, including the wheel! Many of the world's oldest artefacts depict women, and Marija Gimbutas, archeologist of Old Europe, claims that there is no evidence of a father figure in the oldest known historical human era, the paleolithic era (Gimbutas, 1990: 316).

In addition, there is an enormous range of traditional stories from around the world that point to a time when women had much more sacred and secular power than now. Much of early human history is guess work and is limited by the imaginations of people engaged in deciphering it. Three sets of footprints across a volcanic ash plain in Africa may be interpreted as a group of men or a nuclear family, but rarely is it suggested that it may be a group of women. There is no reason for that other than our own prejudices. Likewise human figurines previously interpreted as male are now being relooked at and reinterpreted. Closer to our own time, many cultures have a range of tales about heroines who performed remarkable feats of physical or intellectual strength. This book, in part, is intended to bring to the fore some of this knowledge. All the questions are based on previously published material and shortcomings may be the result of earlier distortion of texts relating to women.

The first thing to say, with regard to the questions asked is, don't feel bad if you don't know the answers. There are many questions about history, the arts, science and women's lives that simply are not part of the mainstream from which educationalists draw their facts. Some of the questions, if you were to look up a male-centred reference book, would either not appear, or have a different answer. This discrepancy is due, not to mischievousness on my part, but rather to the distortion of knowledge about women that prevails in our culture. A great deal of information about women has been lost or destroyed over the generations. The burning of the great library in Alexandria in the first century AD was one of the first great losses. The greater part of Sappho's poetry was lost when the church fathers burnt her work as the works of a heretic. Much more was lost during the years of the witchburnings in Europe. In some instances the losses were not irrevocable. The works of women remained on library shelves gathering dust and have, in recent years, been picked up and read again by feminist scholars in countries all around the world. As a result there is a great deal of re-evaluation of human history from its earliest beginnings going on. But new knowledge takes time to percolate through a culture. In spite of the re-assessment, the caveman image still predominates in the popular imagination, as do many other false images of women.

Have you ever been asked, 'Where are all the great women composers / artists / inventors / scientists / explorers / philosophers / doctors / economists?' The problem with this kind of question is that if you don't have a quick answer, then it is assumed that there were none. There have always been women working at the forefront of just about every human occupation – even those with which we might not want to identify – such as military expertise. Indeed, this is one area where many women's names appear in the records. Sometimes a man has been credited with, say, a work of art, because the person (probably another man) couldn't believe, or did not wish to believe, that a woman could paint so well. At other times men were given credit, because they were the public figures associated with the discovery which they could not have achieved without assistance, without mathematical skill, or without the daily support of a woman. The Japanese poet Sei Shonagon described the sentiment of many women when she wrote:

Very Tiresome Things: When a poem of one's own, that one has allowed someone else to use as his, is singled out for praise.

Even more tiresome were the times when men stole, outright, women's work, thereby establishing lucrative reputations for themselves. Who knows that it was women who invented the basic tools for our contemporary computer society?

When you are asked such a question it is helpful to know a book that contains the answers to these questions. The questions and answers in *The Spinifex Book of Women's Answers* will go some way towards changing the popular conception of what women have, or have not, achieved. The book by no means includes every woman of achievement – many volumes would be needed for that. Some of the questions are phrased in such a way as to make it possible to guess at an answer – there being more information in the question than in the answer. This had been done to help allay the over-whelming feeling of not knowing the answers. Anyone who can answer correctly more than ten percent of the questions is doing well at countering their conditioning and their education.

Amongst the traditions dealt with in this book are also new ones: contemporary feminist traditions. Just as women's work has not been adequately passed on previously, contemporary feminists are concerned to ensure their work is recorded and remembered. Books, art works, political stances and famous utterances are included in this area.

This book can be used in many ways. You can sit down and read it straight through (you will find the answers at the end of each section). You can use it as the basis for a quiz night – a quiz night all about women, or if it's a mixed quiz, as a way of evening up the odds. A question about a famous sportsman should be balanced with one about a famous sportswoman, and so on. The book can be used by students and teachers, as the basis for games or as a source of information about what women have achieved throughout history and in the modern world. Girls need to know about women who have been mathematicians, poets, mechanics, politicians and many other things besides. We all need to know more about our very long history. How does it change a woman's view of herself when she hears that female figures created the world, or that a woman excelled at the same chosen occupation?

Clearly, for an edition published in Australia, questions about Australia and other English-speaking cultures predominate. I have, however, included questions about many other cultures and about women from countries around the world. This does, of course, make it even harder – but not for everyone. These questions will be easier, no doubt, for some. What I have discovered in putting this book together is that what is obscure for one person is very obvious for another. Each of us has our own special interests and this applies to me as the compiler of the questions. I would be interested in hearing from readers who are able to provide questions in areas that are presently under-represented. It is also important to acknow-ledge and rectify the cultural misrepresentation of European-centred history. Many, so-called 'European' cultural institutions were imported from Africa, the Middle East and Asia. Likewise, many oral traditions from around the world record historical events in religious ritual or storytelling form. Some of these oral traditions predate written historical records. Inevitably, however, some areas will not have been adequately covered.

The questions in the book are divided into six categories: Science and Spirit, Herstory, Lives, Time and Place, Ideology, Sport and Culture. The categories provide a focus for questions, but they are not meant to be limiting and you will also find questions about Sport or Science in categories such as Lives or Ideology. Similarly there are occasions when the answers may be incomplete, where, for instance just a few names are listed and the list could be extended. This is not always a quiz about right and wrong answers – there are still many areas where our knowledge is incomplete. Feel free to add your own answers to questions such as, Which goddesses are credited with creating the world? There are too many to list, and if I were to attempt it there would still be omissions. And there are cultures where the names of deities cannot be pronounced – I hope I have not inadvertently overstepped any boundaries in this regard. There are other questions where different traditions provide different answers, and where I have discovered this to be the case, as with immunization and the origin of the Amazons, I have included the variant answers.

The Sources represent those books which were the source of at least three questions or critical new information. Some provided many more. In general, they provide further reading or information on many of the questions. I hope that this book inspires you to read more about the lives and achievements of the women in it.

Susan Hawthorne
August 1991.

Science and Spirit

1. What feature is common to the mythography of the following cultures: the Chibcha people of Colombia, the Finns, the El Salvadorans, the Pelasgians of Ancient Greece, the Etruscans of ancient Italy, the people of Çatal Hüyük in ancient Anatolia (Turkey), the Maori of New Zealand, the Ashanti of Ghana, the Japanese?

2. When brother William was away from home she managed to discover eight comets over the period 1786–1797. She had also discovered three new nebulae in 1793. Brother William was also unwilling to devote the labour and time required to make a proper index that traced and cross-referenced the discrepancies between the official observations and those of the sister/brother team. The result was the *Catalogue of Stars*, recommended by William to his 'Sister to undertake the arduous task'. Who was the sister?

3. In which field of medicine did the Greek physician, Aspasia, contribute the most?

4. What was the cause of 'child bed fever '/'puerperal fever ' during the 19th century?

5. She founded the Sisters of St Joseph of the Sacred Heart and is one of the few Australians to be put forward as a candidate for canonization. What is her name?

6. Name two goddesses from any culture credited with the invention of culture, arts, science, language.

7. Maria Edgeworth (1768–1849), Anglo-Irish novelist who wrote works such as *Belinda* (1801), *Patronage* (1814) and *Helen* (1834), also developed an educational science curriculum for girls and pursued her own scientific interests. In which scientific discipline did she do most of her work?

8. The high-level universal computer programming language, ADA, is named after which English mathematician?

9. What do the pill, the Dalkon Shield, DES, fertility drugs and RU 486 (the French abortion pill) all have in common?

10. Known as the 'Witch of Agnesi', by the age of eleven she was known as the 'Seven-Tongued Orator ' because she spoke fluently Italian, Latin, French, Greek, Hebrew, German and Spanish. She developed a reputation as a scholar in logic, physics, minerology, chemistry, botany, zoology and ontology. In 1738, at the age of twenty, she published *Propositiones philosophicae* and soon announced that she would enter a convent (mostly in order to escape the requirements of secular life, such as fashion, dancing and theatre). Unfortunately Agnesi, despite her reputation, abandoned the area of study in which she showed most promise. Had she continued she would have been considered one of the greatest in her field in the 18th century. What was her field?

11. Aphra Behn, best known for her contribution to literature, translated a scientific work in which field?

12. Amalie Dietrich (1821–1891) wrote *Australische Briefe*. In what field did she work?

13. What do the following madonnas found in European churches have in common? Our Lady of the Hermits at Einsiedeln, Switzerland; Our Lady of Montserrat in Spain; Notre Dame of Kazan in Russia; Our Lady of Czestochowa in Poland; Notre Dame of Hal near Brussels in Belgium; Madonna of Eastern Europe, Monastery Hurezi;   the Madonna of Loretto, Italy; and the Queen of the Pyrenees of Nuria, Spain.

14. A mathematical theorem is named after her which is still considered important by mathematicians. It deals with partial differential equations. The mathematician is Russian. Who is she?

15. In 1967, twenty-four-year-old Jocelyn Bell Burnell noticed an unknown signal from outer space. What discovery did her observations lead to?

16. Alexa Canady said to her parents: 'You're raising me to be the person that you don't want my brothers to marry.' Which profession was Alexa Canady the first black American woman to break into?

17. In what way did Amélie Lelande assist Michel Jean Jérôme Lefrançais de Lelande and Joseph Jérôme Lefrançais de Lelande in their astronomical research?

18. Who did Einstein's mathematics?

19. Hanna Neumann was the first woman to become a professor of what discipline in Australia?

20. Which medieval abbess and healer recommended treating diabetes by omitting sweets and nuts from the diet?

21. Isabella Cunio co-invented which printing method in the 13th century?

22. Scottish-born scientist, Mary Somerville, in her book *On the Connexion of Physical Sciences* presents an important antecedent to the concept of conservation of energy. In the third edition of the same work she wrote that an analysis of the perturbations of Uranus might yield the orbit of an unseen planet. Her work spread the idea and led to the discovery of which planet?

23. Hertha Marks Ayerton in 1904 read a paper on 'The Origin and Growth of Ripple Marks' to the Royal Society (the Royal Society is the most prestigious scientific society in Britain). How many other women had done this previously?

24. Who disproved the theory of phlogiston as it was applied to combustion?

25. Eleanor Omerod began collecting beetles as a child. In which field did she excel in later life?

26. Who was the first major sanitation engineer who, for this task, did not carry a lamp?

27. What feature is common to the mythography of the following cultures: the Ona of Tierra del Fuego, the Aboriginal people of Arnhem Land in Northern Australia, the indigenous people of the Amazon Basin in Brazil, Slavic peoples of USSR, the Songhoi people of the Sudan and many other places?

28. What do the following goddesses have in common: Inanna, Ishtar, Nerthus, Hygeia, Panacea, Scabies, Angina, Fecunditas, Mater Matuta?

29. Trotula is the author of the world's most enduring treatise on what aspect of medicine?

30. Who was the woman to import cinchona bark, as a remedy for malaria, into Spain in the 17th century?

31. About which subject was the first manuscript known to be written by a woman in English, and published in 1671 by Jane Sharp?

32. 'Are not philosophers, mathematicians, and astrologers often inferior to country women in their divinations and predictions, and does not the old nurse very often beat the door?' This was said by physician Agrippa von Nettesheim in which century?

33. Wise women had used the foxglove plant as a remedy for failing heart, irregular heart rhythm, and fluid retention and swelling in legs and feet (dropsy) for centuries (millenia?). What did the eighteenth-century Dr William Withering claim to have discovered about foxglove after visiting an old woman herbalist?

34. Where is the earliest known form of immunization found?

35. In the Sung Dynasty (960–1279 AD), Taoist nuns invented which kind of innoculation for small pox?

36. Who am I? I travelled to Turkey with my husband – the British Ambassador to Constantinople – in 1717. There I learnt how to innoculate against smallpox, a practice I introduced to Britain on my return. This 'new' treatment came in for great criticism from both the medical establishment and from the Church, and I wrote a good deal defending it and myself. 'I am best known, however, for my witty, ascerbic letters that were considered both feminist and funny. Alexander Pope and I were not the best of friends'.

37. With what part of the body is hysteria traditionally associated?

38. Margaret Sanger was born in the late 19th century, and most of her work was done in the early decades of this century. What was her work?

39. Melanie Klein is famous for her psychoanalytic works on the relationship between. . . ?

40. Which company was successfully boycotted by women around the world for its promotion/selling of infant milk formula to Third World countries – a practice that resulted in many thousands of infant deaths due to malnutrition?

41. Mother Theresa worked in which Indian city?

42. Which Indian goddess is Calcutta named after?

43. Who was the Jewish goddess of wisdom?

44. Margaret Mead is best known for her anthropological study of which people?

45. Why did Eve eat the apple?

46. Maria Mitchell was the first woman to be elected to the American Academy of Arts and Sciences, and she said as death approached in 1889, 'Well, if this is dying, there is nothing very unpleasant about it.' In which area of science was she highly regarded?

47. One mathematician devised the formulations for several concepts found in Einstein's theory of relativity; in her work on the theory of ideals she profoundly changed the appearance of algebra; and finally she contributed substantially to work in non-commutative algebras. A school of mathematics is named after her. Who was she?

48. In which field has Norma Merrick Sklarek distinguished herself?

49. What do the following groupings of names have in common?
Parvati–Durga–Uma (Kali) in India; Ana–Babd–Macha (the Morrigan) in Ireland; Hebe–Hera–Hecate, the Moerae, the Gorgons, the Greae, the Horae in Greece; the Norns among the Vikings; the Fates or Fortunae among the Romans; Al-Lat–Q're–Al-Uzza (Manat) among those of Arabia; Diana Triformis among the Druids.

50. Who said in 1764: 'There have been very learned women as there have been women warriors, but there have never been women inventors.' ?

51. Who did the Greeks claim as the inventor of agriculture and the mechanical arts?

52. The Indian goddess, Sarasvati is credited with what inventions?

53. In the 11th century Trotula devised a surgical technique for which operation?

54. Marie Colinet, a Swiss physician of the 16th century was the first to remove iron fragments from the eye with what instrument?

55. Seventy years before its 'discovery' Elizabeth Stone working with lumberjacks in the North Woods of Wisconsin used which antibiotic therapy?

56. Anne Crépin of France invented what kind of saw?

57. Mme Lefebvre patented the first process for fixing which gas from the air?

58. What do the following have in common? Scotchgard, Liquid Paper, the first business computer, the fungicide Nystatin, the first on-line reservation system for airlines?

59. Bette Graham invented what essential item for writers and secretaries?

60. Who is credited with inventing the wheel?

61. Eli Whitney previously credited with inventing the spinning wheel and Albert Einstein with the theory of relativity shared what with Catherine Greene and Mileva Maric-Einstein respectively?

62. Fritz Haber received the Nobel Prize for Chemistry in 1918 for a technology whose earliest form was developed and patented by a woman from Paris. What is her name?

63. Margaret Bourke-White, an American photographer of the 1920s and 30s photographed what kind of subjects?

64. Marie Chambefort was one of the earliest French photographers producing her work in the first decade of photography's existence had previously worked in what kind of printing job?

65. In May 1839 an English woman, Constance Talbot, was setting what she called her husband's 'mousetraps'. What art form were these 'mousetraps' to begin?

66. Anna Atkins made photograms of botanical specimens on light-sensitive paper, making them visually recognizable. In 1843 she published the first photographically illustrated book, *Photographs of British Algae*. The photographs were blue. What process did she use?

67. Rosalie Bertell's book, *No Immediate Danger* is a book about what environmental problem?

68. Who am I? My father was the poet Lord Byron. My mother's marriage to him lasted only a few months. My mother was a mathematical whizz. I was a sickly child, but my mother ensured I received an excellent education, especially in mathematics. In the early 1830s I met Charles Babbage. Together we worked on the programs and mechanics of the world's first computer. I wrote a great deal about my work, but signed it only with initials (ladies didn't write their full name!).

69. What Australian artist produced many woodcuts of Australian wild-flowers?

70. Caroline Louisa Atkinson and Louisa Anne Meredith were both 19th century Australian novelists.What else did they have in common?

71. What was the fruit which Persephone ate that prevented her from fully leaving the Underworld?

72. What is the female part of a flower called?

73. Whose botanical paintings from travels to Brazil, North America, Japan, Sarawak, Australia, the Seychelles, Chile and elsewhere are on permanent display in a special building in Kew Gardens, London?

74. Caroline Herschel made which instrument necessary for the eventual sighting of Uranus?

75. *A Compendius System of Astronomy* was published in 1797 in London. Who was the author?

76. Jane Marcet wrote a book that stimulated the enthusiasm of Michael Faraday. In which field of science did she work?

77. Who was the marine biologist whose work on pesticides helped to bring public attention to ecological issues in the 1960s?

78. What did Mary say when she found she was pregnant?

79. What was the name of the woman God made before making Eve?

80. When the Olympic Games finally got off the ground in the 8th century BC, what kind of priestess had to be present at the men-only Games?

81. The goddess Freya from Norway gives us which day of the week?

82. The Greek goddess Aphrodite is represented by what planet?

83. What is Cassandra remembered for?

84. Who wrote: 'The entire history of science is a progression of exploded fallacies, not of achievements.' ?

85. Which American writer is known for teaching a stone to talk and being a pilgrim at Tinker's Creek?

86. Helen Caldicott is continuing a life-long campaign against which worldwide health hazard ?

87. What Australian woman is responsible for the development of the merino sheep?

88. Dian Fossey is to mountain gorillas as Cynthia Moss is to . . . ?

89. What was the name of the IUD that caused many problems for women, and for which its company was ordered to make large pay-outs as compensation?

90. Adrienne Rich wrote: She died / a famous woman / denying / her sounds / denying / her wounds / came / from the same source as her power Which famous scientist is she writing about?

91. What was it that Marie Curie discovered?

92. Rosalind Franklin's work was critical in the discovery of an impor-tant aspect of modern science. Maurice Wilkins was given the Nobel Prize for work it is widely believed she had done. What was Rosalind Franklin's contribution to science?

93. This scientist could have written the history of each of her corn plants. She said herself, 'I know them intimately, and I find it a great pleasure to know them.' She was awarded the Nobel Prize for her important work on these same corn plants. What was her name?

94. From which African goddess did the Virgin Mary borrow many of her attributes, including her titles: The Madonna, Queen of Heaven, Mother of God, The Great Mother, Our Lady?

95. What do the following writers all have in common: Gertrude the Great, Juliana of Norwich, Birgitta of Sweden, Catherine of Sienna, Hadewych of Antwerp, Beatrice of Nazareth, Hildegard of Bingen?

96. What were New Orleans women, Sanité Dédé, Marie Saloppé and Marie Laveau famous for?

97. Betty de Bono worked as a Union Delegate at Taubmans paint factory in the Western suburbs of Melbourne. What did she work to change in her workplace?

98. Which American comedian said: 'If you have a psychotic fixation and you go to the doctor and you want these two fingers amputated,

he will not cut them off. But he *will* remove your genitals. I have more trouble getting a prescription for Valium than I do having my uterus lowered and made into a penis.' ?

99. What happened after German runner, Lina Radke, won the 800m in 1928?

100. According to Plutarch, Sappho invented a musical scale, the myxolydian mode, built upon the fifth note of the Western scale. According to Plutarch, which emotion is aroused by the myxolydian mode?

101. Ida P. Rolf (1896–1979) writes that the body is not healed only by chemistry but also by attention to structure and physics. What hands-on technique did she invent?

102. What animal product was used in the construction of corsets?

103. Who had a spin-off to prove who was the best weaver? What was the result?

104. For what masculine evils was Pandora blamed?

105. Which Indian Goddess is known as the Dark Mother?

106. Which zodiac sign is symbolized by a woman?

107. Which people worshipped the goddess Cerridwen?

108. In which part of the world do the Djangguwal Sisters and the Wawalag Sisters travel?

Science and Spirit – Answers

1. That a female deity created the world.

2. Caroline Herschel.

3. Obstetrics and gynaecology.

4. Caused by spreading of bacteria, frequently by physicians who did not wash their hands after examining cadavers and who then went straight to the bedside of a woman about to deliver and carried out digital examinations. The highest rates were in large lying-in hospitals, 160 per 1000 live births in England in 1872 (almost 1 in 5!). Midwives had much lower mortality rates.

5. Mary MacKillop.

6. Miti-Miti (Siberian Koryaks), Tsenabonapil (Melanesian New Ireland), Sarasvati (India), Athena (Greece), Minerva (Roman), Brigit (Ireland), Isis (Egypt).

7. Astronomy.

8. (Augusta) Ada Byron Lovelace (1815–52).

9. They all have short- and long-term adverse effects on women's bodies.

10. Mathematics, her major publication was *Analytical Institutions*. Her real name was Maria Gaetana Agnesi.

11. Astronomy. She translated Bernard le Bovier de Fontanelle's *Entretiens sur la pluralité des mondes*.

12. She was a naturalist.

13. They are all black.

14. Sonya Kovalevsky, a creative mathematician of the highest order. The mathematical theorem is the Cauchy-Kovalevsky theorem.

15. Pulsars. Her supervisor received a Nobel Prize for *his* work.

16. She is a neurosurgeon.

17. She did the calculation of astronomical tables.

18. Mileva Maric-Einstein (his wife).

19. She was the inaugural Chair in Pure Mathematics in 1964 at Australian National University.

20. Hildegard of Bingen.

21. Woodblock engraving, co-invented with her brother Alexander.

22. Neptune. Mary Somerville and Caroline Herschel were the first women awarded honorary membership in the Royal Society.

23. None, she was the first. They were ripple marks in sand.

24. Elizabeth Fulhame, a British chemist. Her work was entitled *Essay on Combustion* and she is significant in not only applying empirical methods but also in developing theoretical explanations for her observations.

25. Entomology; she wrote several important books about British insects, with particular reference to their effect on agriculture.

26. Florence Nightingale – she designed many sanitation systems in India, and is particularly well known for that in Delhi.

27. That there was a time when women held the sacred power and were the rulers of the culture.

28. All were associated with healing.

29. Gynaecology and obstetrics.

30. The Countess of Cinchon. She had previously been cured by its use while in Peru, and presumably was given the remedy by the peoples native to that area, again probably women.

31. It concerned midwifery and was called *The Midwives' Book*.

32. Sixteenth century.

33. That foxglove was useful for the above ailments. He wrote a paper entitled 'An Account of the Foxglove and Some of Its Medical Uses' thereby establishing a reputation as one of the finest botanists of all time!

34. In Africa, through the process of cicatrization (scarring) the body is stimulated to create anti-bodies. It is likely that this was the purpose in all cultures that traditionally include scarification.

35. Variolation – innoculation with smallpox virus rather than milder cowpox virus.

36. Lady Mary Wortley Montague.

37. Uterus.

38. She fought to set up women's health centres to help educate women about contraception and reproductive health.

39. Mother and child.

40. Nestlé.

41. Calcutta.

42. Kali.

43. Sophia.

44. Samoa.

45. She wanted to have eternal knowledge.

46. Astronomy. In 1849 she became a computer for the *American Ephemeris and Nautical Almanac*.

47. Amalie Emmy Noether; mathematicians speak of the 'Noether school' of mathematics.

48. Architecture, she designed Terminal One at Los Angeles International Airport.

49. Some of the original Trinity of the goddess in the Indo-european world.

50. Voltaire.

51. Athena.

52. Wisdom, science, speech, music and the deviser of Sanskrit script.

53. Perineal repair.

54. The magnet.

55. Penicillin.

56. The bandsaw.

57. Nitrogen.

58. They were all invented or co-invented by women in the 20th century.

59. Liquid Paper.

60. Athena/Minerva; she was credited with inventing the cart, and in order to have a cart one must have wheels.

61. Royalties.

62. Mme Lefebvre in 1859.

63. Industrial imagery and documentary magazine work.

64. As a daguerreotypist.

65. Photography.

66. Cyanotype.

67. Low-level radiation.

68. Ada Byron Lovelace.

69. Margaret Preston.

70. Both were botanists.

71. The pomegranate.

72. Gynoecium.

73. Marianne North (1830–90).

74. The mirror for the 30-foot reflector of the telescope.

75. Margaret Bryan.

76. Chemistry and the book was called *Conversations on Chemistry.*

77. Rachel Carson.

78. 'How can this be, seeing I know not a man.' (Luke, 1:34).

79. Lilith.

80. A priestess of Demeter.

81. Friday.

82. Venus.

83. She made prophecies but was not believed.

84. Ayn Rand (1905–1982) in her book *Atlas Shrugged.*

85. Annie Dillard, the titles of her books (two of them) are *Teaching a Stone to Talk* and *Pilgrim at Tinker's Creek.*

86. Nuclear War / power.

87. Elizabeth Macarthur.

88. Elephants.

89. The Dalkon Shield.

90. Marie Curie.

91. Radium / radiation.

92. She contributed to the discovery of the DNA structure.

93. Barbara McClintock.

94. Isis.

95. All were mystics and philosophers during the middle ages in Europe.

96. They were voodoo queens.

97. Safety regulations. She died at the age of forty-seven, probably from inhaling dangerous fumes.

98. Lily Tomlin, 1974.

99. The distance was declared dangerous for women and removed from the Olympic calendar for thirty-six years.

100. Passion.

101. Rolfing – a technique that allows emotional residue held in the muscles, and thereby affecting movement through skeletal and muscular tension, to be released.

102. Whalebone.

103. Arachne challenged Athene / the goddess turned her into a spider.

104. War, death, disease, etc.

105. Kali.

106. Virgo.

107. Celts.

108. Central and Northern Australia.

Herstory

109. The bones of 'Lucy', the earliest known human, were found where?

110. Which religions does archeologist, Marija Gimbutas, claim to be the first religions?

111. What is the oldest known representation of the human body?

112. Who was the first known writer in the world?

113. At around 1000 BC and earlier, women-only Games were held in Greece, and were probably the source of the idea for the Olympic Games. What were the Games called?

114. What was the title of the first novel in the world? Who wrote it?

115. Who wrote thirteen novels thirty years before Daniel Defoe wrote what is usually referred to as the 'first novel', *Robinson Crusoe*?

116. She was the first woman to write for publication in her own name. She wrote the first public letters, the first biography of a husband, the first autobiography, the first science fiction as well as major scientific and philosophical works.

117. The current custodians of the good name of Samuel Pepys have taken legal advice to see if it is possible to defame a dead man. How has this great British diarist and idol been brought into disrepute?

118. Who invented hieroglyphs?

119. In what way were the ancient Queens of Ethiopia different from their Egyptian sisters?

120. Known by the names of Makeda or Belkis, and ruler for fifty years over areas as widely separated as Upper Egypt, Armenia, Arabia, Ethiopia, India and Syria. By what name is she known in the *Bible*, the *Koran,* the *Talmud* and in the traditional stories of Syria, Israel, Egypt and Ethiopia?

121. Who built the third pyramid at Giza, Egypt?

122. Djamila Bouhared and Djamila Boupacha were involved in the Algerian resistance movement in the 50s? What were they famous for?

123. For what is the Burmese queen Mallica remembered?

124. Who said, defending her people against the Romans: 'It will not be the last time, Britons, that you have been victorious under the conduct of your queen. For my part, I come here as one descended of royal blood, not to fight for empire or riches, but as one of the common people, to avenge the loss of their liberty, the wrongs of myself and children.'?

125. Ireland and Scotland are named after whom?

126. Bouboulina, a Greek heroine of the 19th century was famous for what?

127. The Mexican woman La Malinche is famous for what?

128. Which country did Cut Nyak Dien rule for fifty years in the 17th century?

129. I was born in 1583 and known variously as Jinga or Ginga, but more ofter as Nzingha. I was the sister of King Ndongo, Ngoli Bbondi and belonged to the people known as the Jagas. The Portuguese attempted to enslave my people, so I made an alliance with the Dutch. In 1623 at the age of forty-one I became Queen of Ndongo and when leading the army I wore male attire. I became known as a visionary political leader and one committed to resistance to European invasion. The Portuguese captured and beheaded my sister, Fungi. I joined the Catholic faith because of the power of its god and signed a treaty with the Portuguese. In 1663 when I was nearing eighty, I died. After my death the Portuguese enslaved South West Africa. What is the modern-day name for my country?

130. I am called the Falasha Queen, and unlike my African sisters Candace and Nzingha, I didn't simply defend my country, I challenged and fought and defeated the Abyssinian Solomonid dynasty and then reigned unchallenged for forty years. I did not like Christians and so I destroyed their churches and their people. The world still does not know all there is to know about me. What is my name?

131. Who was the leader of the Ashanti people in Ghana against the British in the early years of the twentieth century?

132. In which country did the Ibu Women's War of 1929 take place?

133. Which members of the Yoruba culture (Nigeria) traditionally wore plaits?

134. In 40 AD the Trung Sisters, Trung Trai and Trung Nhi, led the first national insurrection against the Chinese. Which modern-day nation were the Trung Sisters defending?

135. Christine de Pisan wrote the following lines about a French heroine. Who was she writing about? 'O Thou! ordained Maid of very God! / Joanna! born in Fortune's golden hour'

136. For what crime was Joan of Arc tried?

137. Help from whom was indispensable to Jason getting the Golden Fleece?

138. Who is the Catherine wheel named after?

139. When a woman was burnt 'quick' after being accused and found guilty of witchcraft, what did that mean?

140. The book which provided the basic material for accusations of witchcraft against many a good feminist was called the *Malleus Maleficarum*. What was its English title/translation?

141. Who is said to have been the first great alchemist?

142. Which novelist was the first woman named to the prestigious 'Academie Française'?

143. *The Mists of Avalon* by Marion Bradley tells the history of which culture?

144. What is the name of the woman who features in Kate Grenville's fictional history of Australia?

145. Mary Grant Bruce is best known for her series of novels featuring a young heroine named Norah Linton. The series is called . . . ?

146. Which novel by Catherine Helen Spence is one of the first books about Australia by a woman, as well as being an important record of life in South Australia and the Victorian goldfields in the 19th century?

147. Who set up the first all-female garage in Melbourne in 1919?

148. Who was the first Aboriginal woman to be appointed Magistrate?

149. In 1956 Pearl and Faith established the Australian Aboriginal Fellowship. What are their last names?

150. Who was responsible in 1946 for Aboriginal workers at Roy Hill in Western Australia going on strike and for the subsequent spread of the strike to the Pilbara region further inland? The strike changed the structure of labour relations in the north of the state forcing many stations to recognize that wages would have to be raised.

151. Who wrote the first novel written and printed in Australia and what was it called?

152. Tasmanian, Constance Stone, the first woman to become a practising doctor in Melbourne started the Queen's Shilling Fund to set up what institution to be run by women for women in 1897?

153. Elizabeth Garrett Anderson was the first woman to be admitted to the previously all-male British Medical Association. In which year was she admitted?

154. What public office was Elizabeth Garrett Anderson the first to hold in England?

155. Olympe de Gouges wrote the *Declaration of the Rights of Women* in 1791. What was the title of Mary Wollstonecraft's book on the same subject published in 1792?

156. Who started the Russian Revolution with the cry: 'Bread and Roses'?

157. What is 'General' Harriet Tubman famous for?

158. Who said: 'But ain't I a woman?'

159. How was news of secret meetings for Black women passed from one end of a city, such as New Orleans, during the slave era in the USA?

160. Who created the Women's Social and Political Union (WSPU) in Britain?

161. Who sparked the civil rights movement in the USA by refusing to go to the back of the bus?

162. Who became the first woman premier of Victoria?

163. Who began working in a mill at the age of ten, and later became a leader in the British Suffrage movement?

164. What was the best-selling novel in nineteenth-century America?

165. With which international crisis are the photographs of Dorothea Lange associated?

166. A law affecting the extermination of what people did Esther convince her husband to repeal?

167. Who said: 'The serpent beguiled me and I did eat?' (Genesis, 3:13)

168. After cutting off the head of Holofernes she said: 'Her sandal ravished his eye, / her beauty took his soul prisoner. . . / and the scimitar cut through his neck!' Who was speaking?

169. Who painted two pictures in 17th century Italy of Judith cutting off Holofernes' head?

170. Who said on the day of her death: 'I have heard say the executioner is very good, and I have a little neck.'?

171. One of the greatest rulers of Egypt was a woman. She was called Pharaoh and was a warrior queen, though she waged no wars abroad. She organized commercial expeditions and is credited with creating a new science of rulership. She is depicted wearing a beard. What is her name?

172. Cleopatra, the black ruler of Egypt committed suicide soon after Mark Antony's death. Her loss of him is usually said to be the reason for her suicide. What was the real reason?

173. Who was the next queen the Romans had to contend with after the death of Cleopatra?

174. Margaret of Austria (1480–1530) was Regent of what country?

175. 'Everyone knows that . . . a woman ought not to let it appear that she understands . . .' Who wrote this in *The Heptameron*?

176. Who said the following at her trial in 1586: 'Look to your consciences and remember that the theatre of the world is wider than the realm of England.'?

177. Who did Antoinette de Pons Guercheville (1570–1632) direct the following remark at: 'If I am not noble enough to be your wife, I am too much so to be your mistress.'?

178. On 24 October 1975 there was a 24-hour Women's Strike in one nation. In which country was this strike held?

179. On 14 June 1991 there was a Women's Strike in a European country to protest the existence of 700 years of 'Papiland' (fatherland). In which country was the strike held?

180. In which year did Swiss women get the right to vote federally?

181. In which year did Swiss women in all cantons achieve the right to vote?

182. My birth is recorded as being the daughter of Queen Marie Theresa of Spain and Louis XIV of France. The court was distressed when I was born as I resembled my mother's Dahomian attendant, Nabo. I was taken secretly to the convent of Moret and when I grew up I became known as the Black Nun. When my mother named me she chose to combine my legal parents' names. What is my name?

183. Which suffragette and contraception activist wrote the following words: 'No woman can call herself free who does not own and control her own body.'?

184. On which continent are the earliest-known examples of the following found: wigs, eye shadow, breath freshener, nail stain, lipstick, scented pomades and oils for the skin and hair?

185. Who designed the first mini-skirts?

186. In which year did Robin Morgan and other feminists first disrupt a Miss America contest?

187. In which year were the following three books published:
The Feminine Mystique, The Group, The Bell Jar?

188. In which year were the following books published:
The Dialectic of Sex, The Female Eunuch, Sexual Politics, Sisterhood is Powerful: An Anthology of Writings from the Women's Liberation Movement?

189. In which year was the US feminist magazine, *Ms.* first published?

190. Who were/are the first and current editors of *Ms.* magazine?

191. In which year did the UK feminist magazine, *Spare Rib* begin?

192. What was the name of the newspaper printed by Louisa Lawson and her women-only press?

193. Madame Helena Blavatsky set up which prominent society?

194. C. A. Dawson, known variously as 'Sappho' and 'Mrs Sappho' founded which international organization in 1921?

195. Women's Wax Works recording label produced the first lesbian record recorded and produced by women. What was it called?

196. Which US feminist and woman-owned recording company released work by Meg Christian, Cris Williamson, and Margie Adam?

197. Who published Robin Morgan's first book of poems, *Monster*, in Australia?

198. Which famous American writer and activist wrote the famous words: 'Men, their rights and nothing more; women, their rights – nothing less.'?

199. Which American writer is known for shooting Andy Warhol, and authoring the controversial book *The SCUM Manifesto*?

200. What was the title of Sylvia Plath's most famous novel?

201. Name the seven women writers who have won the Nobel Prize for Literature up to 1992.

202. Who am I? I lived in Saxony sometime between 935–1000 AD. I was the abbess of a Benedictine nunnery. My plays and dramas were respected but ignored for a long time. One of my plays is said to be the earliest version of the *Faust* story.

203. Who ruled the court at Poitiers from 1170 creating an influential centre for art and culture and in particular for the flowering of Troubadour song?

204. The author of *The Tale of Genji* wrote the following: 'Indeed she had seen enough of the world to know that in few people is discretion stronger than the desire to tell a story. . .' What is the writer's name?

205. Known as the first Black poet in the US, who wrote these lines: 'I, young in life, by seeming cruel fate / Was snatched from Afric's fancy'd happy seat: / What pangs excruciating must molest, / What sorrows labor in my parent's breast?'

206. Who was the first black woman to have a play appear on Broadway?

207. Who wrote the first Australian novel about convict life in Tasmania? What was its title?

208. Sue Hardisty wrote the book, and with Susan Maslin, made the documentary, *Thanks Girls and Goodbye*. What aspect of Australian history does it deal with?

209. Who wrote the novel *Bring the Monkey*?

210. Who was the first European woman to cross the Franklin and Jane Rivers in Tasmania?

211. Her first piece of fiction was published in *Vashti's Voice*, a Melbourne feminist newspaper. She was dismissed from her teaching job and her first novel, published in 1977 was set in Melbourne's inner suburbs. Jane Campion directed her script, *Two Friends*, an award-winning telefeature. What is her name?

212. Name the Maori writer who won the Victoria University Writer in Residence Award in 1985, and subsequently won the New Zealand Book Award for her novel, *Potiki*.

213. Which New Zealand children's writer was approached by a New York publisher when she was thirty-two and has since published over forty-five children's books?

214. The name Aoteoroa is applied to which country by its indigenous people?

215. Whom did Aeneas leave in Carthage?

216. Synesius of Cyrene (in North Africa) credited her with the invention of apparatus for distilling water and measuring the level of liquids. She was known for her work in algebra, geometry and astronomy. She was a leading figure in non-Christian thought in Alexandria and in 415 AD she was murdered and dismembered by a mob of Christian fanatics. Who was she?

217. I was born in 1415 BC, daughter of Yuya and Thuya, Nubians and high priests in service of the god Amun. Although neither Egyptian nor royal, I married the Pharaoh Amenhotep III. I was mother to Akhenaten, Smenkhare and Tutankhamen, all Pharaohs. I stabilized Egypt during the 18th dynasty and took over the role of Secretary of State during my sons' reigns. During my reign women prospered and I introduced to Egypt the tradition of matrilineal succession. What is my name?

218. Who was the daughter-in-law of Tiye, renowned for her beauty, intellect and insistence on equality?

219. Byzantium was ruled by which woman in the 6th century AD?

220. Which woman pharaoh built a temple in the Valley of Kings?

221. Who am I? I lived between 1122–1204. My own fame equalled that of my husbands and my sons who became kings of great renown. During my reign I held and administered lands equalling one-third of present-day France, established my own court which was celebrated for its enlightenment and patronage of the arts, and went off to the crusades.

222. In Italy during the 17th century there were many artists who achieved fame for their excellent work. One such woman and her work have only recently received the attention they deserve after being 'forgotten' by the art establishment. What was her name?

223. Which 'Russian Amazon' assassinated Czar Alexander II in 1881?

224. What did the women in the play *Lysistrata* refuse to do?

225. Her sonnets were considered the greatest sonnets since Shakespeare?

226. Who originated the Montessori method?

227. She ran an important artistic salon in Paris during the 1920s, including all-female evenings, who was she?

228. Which French philosopher committed suicide by starvation in 1934?

229. Justice Mary Gaudron was the first woman appointed to what Australian Court in February 1987, in the entire eighty-four years of existence?

230. Who was the first woman Supreme Court Judge, now Governor of South Australia?

231. Who was the first woman ever appointed to the head or deputy head of a Law Reform Commission in Australia?

232. The film *Two Laws* is about women from which Aboriginal community in northern Australia?

233. *My Survival as an Aboriginal* tells the story of whose life?

234. How many feature films were made by women in Australia between 1921 and 1933?

235. Which Chinese poet wrote: 'Why should marriage bring only tears? / All I wanted was a man / With a single heart, / And we would stay together / As our hair turned white, Not somebody always after wriggling fish / With his big bamboo rod.' ?

236. Which ruler of Egypt said the following to Marc Antony: 'Leave the fishing rod, Great-General, to us sovereigns of Pharos and Canopus.' ?

237. What shouldn't you do if you meet Medusa?

109. Hadar, Ethiopia.

110. Goddess religions.

111. The Venus of Willendorf.

112. Enheduanna, 2300 BCE in Sumeria.

113. Herean Games, after the goddess, Hera.

114. *The Tale of Genji* by Murasaki Shikibu.

115. Aphra Behn. (1640–1689).

116. Margaret Cavendish. (1623/4–1673/4).

117. By the publication of *The Diary of Elizabeth Pepys*, edited by Dale Spender, 1991.

118. Seshat, goddess of the written word in Egypt.

119. The Ethiopian Queens were independent rulers; most of the Queens of Egypt gained their stature via the King Pharaoh.

120. Queen of Sheba.

121. Nitocris.

122. Fighting.

123. For killing over fifty military elephants when leading an army in tribal war.

124. Boadicea (also known as Boudicca).

125. Queen Eire and Queen Scota.

126. She was a sea pirate who fought the Turks.

127. She was a skilled linguist, learning Spanish in a matter of weeks and became interpreter for Cortés. Although maligned by historians as a traitor La Malinche managed to save the lives of thousands of Native Indians through her influence over Cortés.

128. Indonesia.

129. Angola.

130. Judith. (Some Ethiopian historical manuscripts have never been released; perhaps when they are we will know more about Judith).

131. Yaa Asantewa.

132. Nigeria.

133. The women.

134. Viet Nam.

135. Joan of Arc.

136. Witchcraft.

137. Medea.

138. St Catherine (Catherine of Sienna).

139. To be burnt 'quick' meant to be burnt alive.

140. *The Hammer of Witches.*

141. The Virgin Mary.

142. Marguerite Yourcenar.

143. Celtic.

144. Joan in *Joan Makes History.*

145. The Billabong Books.

146. *Clara Morison.*

147. Alice Anderson.

148. Pat O'Shane. The first Aboriginal to be appointed to a

Magistrates' Court anywhere is Australia in 1986, she was also the first woman to be appointed to head a government department – Department of Aboriginal Affairs in New South Wales.

149. Pearl Gibbs and Faith Bandler.

150. Daisy Bindi, also known as Mumaring of the Nungamurda people.

151. Anna Maria Bunn, *The Guardian* in 1838.

152. The Queen Victoria Hospital in Melbourne, opened in 1889.

153. 1873.

154. Mayor (of Aldeburgh in 1908).

155. *A Vindication of the Rights of Women.*

156. Women.

157. Leading slaves to freedom from the southern states of the USA.

158. Sojourner Truth.

159. By means of song. Each woman would sing a song with a message attached at the end, the next would repeat the song and pass it on to next door and so it would travel across the city.

160. Emmeline and Christabel Pankhurst.

161. Rosa Parkes.

162. Joan Kirner.

163. Annie Kenney.

164. Harriet Beecher Stowe's *Uncle Tom's Cabin.*

165. The depression of the 1930s.

166. Jewish people.

167. Eve.

168. Judith. (Judith, 16:9).

169. Artemisia Gentileschi.

170. Anne Boleyn (19 May 1536).

171. Hatshepsut.

172. Egypt was a Roman protectorate that Cleopatra protected through liaisons with Roman rulers, Julius Caesar and Mark Antony. Once they were dead Octavius assumed full control of Egypt. Egypt lost any remaining autonomy and Cleopatra committed suicide over the loss of her country, not over the loss of a man.

173. Candace of Ethiopia – there were several queens of this name.

174. Netherlands (Holland).

175. Margaret of Navarre, the book has the alternative title of *Novels of the Queen of Navarre.*

176. Mary, Queen of Scots (1542–87).

177. Henry IV.

178. Iceland.

179. Switzerland.

180. 1971.

181. 1991.

182. Marie-Louise.

183. Margaret Sanger.

184. Africa.

185. Mary Quant.

186. 1968 in Atlantic City.

187. 1963.

188. 1970.

189. 1972.

190. Gloria Steinem / Robin Morgan.

191. 1971.

192. *The Dawn*.

193. The Theosophical Society.

194. PEN.

195. *Lavender Jane Loves Women*.

196. Olivia Records.

197. Radical Feminists.

198. Susan B. Anthony.

199. Valerie Solanas

200. *The Bell Jar*.

201.
Selma Lagerlöf	1909
Grazia Deledda	1926
Sigrid Undset	1928
Pearl S. Buck	1938
Gabriela Mistral	1945
Nelly Sachs (shared)	1966
Nadine Gordimer	1991

202. Hrotsvita of Gandersheim.

203. Eleanor of Aquitaine.

204. Lady Murasaki Shikibu.

205. Phillis Wheatley (1753?–1784).

206. Lorraine Hansberry. The play was *A Raisin in the Sun*.

207. Caroline Woolmer Leakey ('Oliné Keese'). The book was *The Broad Arrow*, the year, 1859.

208. The Women's Land Army which operated during World War II.

209. Miles Franklin.

210. Lady Jane Franklin.

211. Helen Garner.

212. Patricia Grace.

213. Margaret Mahy.

214. New Zealand (it means 'the land of the long white cloud').

215. Dido.

216. Hypatia.

217. Tiye.

218. Nefertiti.

219. Theodora.

220. Hatshepsut.

221. Eleanor of Acquitaine.

222. Artemisia Gentileschi.

223. Sophia Perovskaya.

224. To have sex with men.

225. Elizabeth Barrett Browning.

226. Maria Montessori.

227. Natalie Barney.

228. Simone Weil.

229. High Court of Australia.

230. Dame Roma Mitchell.

231. Jocelynne Scutt, appointed in December 1984.

232. Borroloola.

233. Essie Coffey.

234. Sixteen.

235. Chuo Wên-chün.

236. Cleopatra.

237. Look at her face.

238. What percentage of food by weight do women in sub-arctic gatherer-hunter societies provide?

239. On average in Asia and Africa, how many *more* hours a week than men do women work?

240. I was born in France, though my uncle was President of Peru, and grew up in poverty with my widowed mother. I fought my husband for custody of my children, but I was unable to get a divorce as it was suppressed in France in 1816. My husband later attempted to murder me upon reading my autobiography *Peregrinations d'une paria*. I wrote *Union ouvrière*, the first call for a world union of workers that predated Marx's Manifesto of 1848. I died of typhoid in 1844 in Bordeaux while publicizing my ideas. My grandson, Paul Gauguin later became famous for his paintings. Who am I? Where am I buried?

241. Who said the following: '. . . they [MGM] had us working days and nights on end. They'd give us pep-up pills to keep us on our feet long after we were exhausted. Then they'd take us to the studio hospital and knock us cold with sleeping pills . . . Half the time we were hanging from the ceiling, but it became a way of life for us.'?

242. Who was the first woman film star to make a million dollars?

243. Who said: 'Mary Pickford may have been the first woman to make a million, but I am the first to spend one.'?

244. Who said: 'One can never be too thin or too rich.'?

245. Who said, 'Just remember – you can be too rich.'?

246. One of Hollywood's most famous actresses said: 'I want to be known as an actress. I'm not royalty.' Who was it?

247. How did Olympe de Gouges die?

248. Ten days after my birth on 30 August 1797, my famous mother died. I grew up in Scotland and in 1912 I met a man called Percy with

whom I eloped two years later. Before I was 21 I had completed and published a novel which was to become famous throughout the world, and the basis for many films. I wrote one of the earliest works of fiction about incest, *Mathilde* and my story 'The Last Man' has been widely anthologized. The famous names in my life are Wollstonecraft, Godwin, Shelley and Frankenstein. Who am I?

249. What did Katherine Mansfield die of?

250. In the Brontë family there was a fourth sister who died of consumption at the age of twelve, and who provided the model for Helen Burns in *Jane Eyre*. What was the sister's name?

251. How and at what age did Eleanor Marx die?

252. *Sudden Death* by Rita Mae Brown is based on which famous tennis player?

253. I grew up in Beaumont, Texas, and as a child was prodigiously good at almost any sport I tried. When I was sixteen I had an offer to move to Dallas and play for a basketball team as part of a company. On one day, within three hours, in July 1932 I won the javelin, shot put, baseball throw, long jump, 80 metres hurdles and a tie in the high jump. Two were new world records. I won gold medals in javelin and hurdles and tied in the high jump at the Los Angeles Olympics in 1932, setting records in all three events – I was the first athlete to do that. I later went on to win many golf tournaments. Who am I?

254. Ruth spoke the following to Naomi: 'Intreat me not to leave thee, or to return from following after thee: for whither thou goest, I will go; and where thou lodgest, I will lodge; thy people shall be my people. . .' (Ruth, 1: 16) What relation was Naomi to Ruth?

255. *Poppy*, by Drusilla Modjeska, is a book about which relation?

256. My family name is well known in Victorian Aboriginal circles as many of my descendants have been activists. I was born in 1836 on Preservation Island in Bass Strait. With my husband John I travelled to the Victorian goldfields in 1853 after which we went to live at Coranderrk Aboriginal Station. I gave evidence to the enquiry in 1876 to resist plans to sell the property, but I was forced off the land. Laws about half-castes separated the family several times and eventually I moved to Cummeragunja near the Murray River in New South Wales. Some of my descendants were to walk off this land in later years. Who am I?

257. I was born on 25 December 1933 at Echuca, Victoria, a member of the Yorta-Yorta tribe from the Murray River area. Amongst my ancestors were also the Wurundjeri people of the Melbourne area. When I was a child my family and I walked off the Cummeragunja Station to Mooroopna, and later Shepparton. I went to school in the Good Shepherd Convent in Abbotsford, Melbourne and later worked as a domestic at St Andrews Hospital. I married a Andrew Marimutha, a Malayan Indian, whose name we all shortened. I initiated the setting up of the Aboriginal Health Service and the Aboriginal Legal Service. I also set up Worowa Aboriginal College and later Worawa Primary School for younger children. I am well known for co-authoring the script of *Women of the Sun*. Who am I?

258. Zora Neale Hurston worked as a maid, a librarian, and a teacher. What was her main claim to fame?

259. She was born in Chattanooga, her last name was Smith and she sang the blues. Her first name is . . . ?

260. Leontyne Price had her debut at the Metropolitan Opera House in 1961. How long was the ovation she received for her portrayal of Leonora in *Il Trovatore* on that night?

261. At what age did Libba Cotten, Grammy Award-winning singer, storyteller, composer, begin her performing career?

262. I was born in Paris in 1857 and began composing at the age of eight when I wrote church music. I was famous for my recitals in which I often played my own works. I wrote a ballet, *Callirhoë*, a composition for chorus and orchestra, *Les Amazones*, a flute concerto and over 200 piano pieces. I died in 1944, aged eighty-six. Who am I?

263. I was born in Japan and became an artist. I exhibited an apple in an art gallery with a high price tag. I also produced the solo records *Approximately Infinite Universe* and *Feeling the Space* as well as records with my husband. I wrote a book of poems, *Grapefruit*. My husband was shot in New York City in 1980. Who am I?

264. I was born in Paris in 1915, the daughter of an Italian street singer, Line Marsa, and I was named after Nurse Edith Cavell. At the age of eight I became blind and my grandmother with whom I lived took me on a pilgrimage to Lisieux. By the age of thirteen I could see again. I sang on the streets with my father and in 1935 I began to sing in cabarets. I was nicknamed 'the sparrow' and after the second world war I became famous. I sang songs composed by my favourite

composer, Marguerite Monot, including *L'Etranger, C'est l'amour*, and *Hymne à l'amour*. My most famous song is *Non, je ne regrette rien*. By what name am I known?

265. Who says: '*I enjoy being a girl*'?

266. I was born in Germany in 1915 and made my debut in opera at the Berlin Staatsoper in Parsifal in 1938. I am well known for my Lieder recitals and I appeared almost annually at the Salzburg Festival for twenty-five years. In recent years I have become well known for my master-classes. Who am I?

267. She was the greatest woman pianist of the nineteenth century and lived in Germany. Her name is . . . ?

268. She composed many musical works, but was prevented from performing publicly first by her father, and then by her brother Felix. Her name is . . . ?

269. Who achieves the remarkable feat of taming nine fire lizards in Anne McCaffrey's *Dragonsong*?

270. Who wrote *Gone With the Wind*?

271. Calamity Jane is known for many things, but she also wrote. What was the title of her small collection of letters?

272. I was born in Glasgow, Scotland in 1960. In 1982 I became the first Black collective-member of Sheba Feminist Publishers in London. I was the in-house editor of the anthologies, *A Dangerous Knowing: Four Blackwomen Poets, Charting the Journey*. I have authored two collections of poetry, *As A Blackwoman* and *Zabat: Poetics of a Family Tree*. I am the co-founder, with Lubaina Himid, of Urban Fox Press, the first independent blackwomen's press in Britain. My most recent book is *Passion: Discourses on Blackwomen's Creativity*. Who am I?

273. Who am I? I joined the suffragettes in England and America. I helped form Women's Trade Unions, and I served in a Scottish hospital unit in war zones during WWI. I'm better known for my novels set in Australia, and for my struggle to establish a brilliant career. My name is . . . ?

274. Who am I? I was a feminist, a committed socialist, and an Australian. In 1936 I wrote a novel which offered a daring exploration of female sexuality. I went on to write other books, many of which dealt with the issues of racism. For many years my work was ignored

and it has just been rediscovered by a new generation of feminists, readers and scholars.

275. I was born in 1762 and worked as a cook in Suffolk for Mr Cobbold. When I was unemployed and desperate I dressed in male attire and rode Mr Cobbold's horse to London. I was sentenced to be hanged, but this was commuted to seven years transportation. At first I was not transported, but sent instead to Ipswich jail. I dressed in sailor clothes and escaped over the wall, but I was recaptured. This time I was transported and sent to Sydney where I worked again as a cook and assisted in the delivering of babies. Although I was asked several times to marry I always refused. In 1814 I was granted an absolute pardon. After that I worked my own farm raising sheep, goats and pigs. Who am I?

276. I was born in Lincolnshire, England around 1612. In 1630, aboard the *Arabella* I set out for Massachusetts. I wrote poems about my life, my children and my house which burnt down. I am known as the first American poet. What is my name?

277. Who was the first woman in the US to be nominated for President?

278. Who were the first women to become professional stockbrokers? Sisters, they set up business in New York in 1868 and were extremely successful.

279. Who said: 'Too much of a good thing can be wonderful.'?

280. Who wrote the following in her diary on 22 November, 1963: 'It all began so beautifully. After a drizzle in the morning, the sun came out bright and clear. We were driving into Dallas. In the lead car were President and Mrs Kennedy. . .'?

281. Who said: 'I have seen all, I have heard all, I have forgotten all.'?

282. I was born in Russian Poland in 1870 and my family moved to Warsaw when I was three. Although I was lame, I never lacked confidence in my ideas. I studied philosophy, economics and law in Zürich and married a German. In 1893 I helped form the Social Democratic Party of Poland. I later worked on the socialist newspaper *Vorwärts* and spent time in prison in 1904 and 1905. I wrote an influential pamphlet, *The Mass Strike* and in 1914 a major text on economics, *The Accumulation of Capital*. I strenuously opposed all forms of nationalism as they destroy international solidarity amongst workers. Due to my anti-nationalist beliefs I spent most of the first world war in prison. My work has been described as providing a

unified theory and tactics for the European-wide revolution. After founding the German Communist Party and, following the Spartacist uprising in 1919, I was arrested, interrogated, beaten and shot. My body was thrown into the Landwehr Canal in Berlin and my murderers were acquitted. Who am I?

283. Indian politician, Vijaya Lakshmi Pandit, was president of what international body in 1953?

284. In 19th century Britain Josephine Butler fought for the repeal of which Acts that discriminated against women but took no account of men's role in spreading venereal disease?

285. Ada Evans was the first Australian woman to graduate in law from Sydney University? In what year did she graduate?

286. A well-known figure in Sydney from the mid-twenties to the sixties, she was a voracious reader, often refused to pay cab fares, gave recitations of Shakespeare wearing a green tennis shade. In old age she claimed, 'I have no allergies that I know of, one complex, no delusions, two inhibitions, no neuroses, three phobias, no superstitions and no frustrations.' She is the subject of Kate Grenville's novel, *Lilian's Story*. What is her name?

287. I was born in 1843 in England and when in my late thirties my eyesight began to fail I turned from working with silver, woodcarving and embroidery to gardening. I designed many gardens based on blending colour in the style of French Impressionist painters. I worked for many years with architect Edward Lutyens, designing gardens for his houses. My gardens broke with the Victorian tradition of 'bedding out', and instead were 'wild', extensively using native plants and herbs. I died in 1932. Who am I?

288. Who is the contemporary British photographer who has documented her own breast cancer?

289. Which American photographer famous for her photographs of people during the Depression era said: '. . . being disabled gave me an immense advantage. People are kinder to you. It puts you on a different level than if you go into a situation whole and secure.'?

290. A film was made in the last decade about two European-born Mexican artists – one a painter, the other a photographer. What are their names?

291. Her work has been described as the 'quintessence of the idealizing Victorian frame of mind'. She lived from 1815 to 1879. Her

photographic subjects include Stella Duckworth, Virginia Woolf, Vanessa Bell. Who is she?

292. New York photographer, Lisette Model, through her street photographs provided inspiration for which other New York photographer famous for portraits of people on the margins?

293. In 1937 the English artist, Gluck said of her painting entitled, Medallion, 'We are not an affair – We are husband and wife.' What kind of relationship was it?

294. *Testament of Friendship* (1940) is a biography of Winifred Holtby but also explores the subject of friendship among women. Who was its author? What was her relationship to Winifred Holtby?

295. Who were the three famous women writers who loved each other in various combinations, and whose first names all started with V ?

296. Who is Virginia Woolf's *Orlando* modelled on?

297. Helen Ambrose, a character in Virginia Woolf's *The Voyage Out*, is based on which relative?

298. Sylvia Townsend Warner's lifelong companion was . . . ?

299. What is the pen-name of Alma Routsong?

300. Radclyffe Hall provided a model for many writers. In 1928 Djuna Barnes satirized her and Una Troubridge as Lady Buckand-Baulk and Tilly-Tweed-in-Blood in which book?

301. The following lines are written on whose gravestone: And if God choose / I shall but love thee better / after death. / Una.?

302. Lady Eleanor Butler lived in Llangollen with . . . ?

303. Their cow was called . . . ?

304. What word does Gertrude Stein use as a metaphor for orgasm in *Lifting Belly?*

305. Who wrote *Conversations With Cow*?

306. I was born in Melbourne, Australia and moved to Britain during the 1970s. My first book of poems was *Hecate's Charms*. I have also

written a novel, *Between Friends* and a book on the life and art of Dorothy Richardson. I have written widely on modernist women writers and on lesbian culture and lifestyle. In 1986 I co-authored a collection of poems with Suniti Namjoshi. Who am I?

307. Who said the following to her brother, Cesare, after the murder of her second husband:'. . . my husbands have been very unlucky.'?

308. I was the most distinguished teacher at Salerno, a medieval medical university in Italy. My existence has been denied by several historians in spite of the fact that my manuscripts are held in several European museums. In my day I was referred to as a *magistra medicinae*. I was particularly famous for managing women's health problems and well known as a diagnostician. I treated conditions such as prolapsed uterus, was the first to describe the dermatological manifestations of syphilis and used opiates for pain management. Who am I?

309. Mechtild of Magdeburg lived in an independent community of nuns. By what name were these independent convents known?

310. Maryse Condé, author of *Heremakhonon*, comes from the Antilles. In what language does she write?

311. In *The Odyssey* who says: 'Careless to please, with insolence ye woo!' as she undoes another night's weaving?

312. Which famous 16th century Spanish philosopher and mystic of the Carmelite order said the following: 'We are not angels and we have bodies. To want to become angels while we are still on earth. . . is ridiculous.'

313. I was born in Kent, but spent my childhood in Surinam, Guyana. I married at eighteen, but my husband soon died. At the age of 26, I went to Antwerp as a spy for Charles II, but fell out of favour and ended up in debtors' prison. I was the first woman in the world to support myself on my writing alone. I wrote poems, histories, novels and seventeen plays, including *The Rover* in which one of my characters, Lady Knowall says: 'Can anything that's great or moving be expressed in filthy English.' My novel was called *Oronooko, or the History of the Royal Slave*. Who am I?

314. The greatest name in medieval Dutch literature was probably also a beguine and possibly the head of a beguinage. She wrote poems that are complex mystical visions. What was her name?

315. By what name were Maria Isabel Barreno, Maria Fatima Velho da Coata and Maria Teresa Horta collectively known?

316. I was born near Barcelona in 1908 and became involved in the Surrealist movement. I was forced into exile when the fascists took over in Spain and in 1940 I was arrested and interned in a French concentration camp. I later left Marseilles as a refugee and arrived in Mexico City at the end of 1941. I worked closely with my friend, Leonora Carrington. My paintings play with the transformation of the ordinary into the extraordinary and include works such as *Embroidering Earth's Mantle, Creation of Birds, Solar Music*. Who am I?

317. In what musical art form did Peggy Glanville-Hicks work?

318. Who loved a sunburnt country?

319. Australia's best known Aboriginal poet is the author of *We Are Going, The Dawn is at Hand, My People* and *Stradbroke Dreaming*. What is her name?

320. What is the name of the book by Katherine Susannah Pritchard that centres on the life of an Aboriginal woman?

321. Which writer left Australia and lived for many years on the Greek island of Hydra?

322. Who am I? I was born in England and later came to Australia. My family ran a Quaker home for down-and-outs. I worked as a nurse, a real-estate agent and a teacher. My manuscripts were rejected for many years. I am now considered one of Australia's finest writers. My name is . . . ?

323. Which novelist was born in Persia, grew up on a farm in Southern Rhodesia and moved to England in 1949?

324. George Eliot is to Mary Anne Evans as Isak Dinesen is to . . . ? and Henry Handel Richardson is to . . . ?

325. Ruth Rendell also writes as . . . ?

326. Hercule Poirot is to Agatha Christie as Adam Dalgliesch is to . . . ?

327. Everyone knows her pen-name, but what was George Sand's real name?

328. Henry James had a sister who was also a writer. Her name was . . . ?

329. My name is Mira, and I'm friends with Val, Isolde, Kyla, Clarissa and Grete. We all appear in which novel?

330. Which woman writer created:

Lola Blau	Sybylla Melvyn
Mrs Ramsay	Louie Pollitt
Kezia	Evelina
Miss Peabody	Fadette
Snugglepot	Maggie Tulliver
Squeaker's mate	Emma

331. *Angel at My Table* is the second volume of Janet Frame's autobiography. What are the titles of the first and third volumes?

332. My forebears are Orcadian, Lancashire and Maori. I worked in Woolworths, as well as being a fish and chip cook, a postie, a tobacco picker, a journalist and trainee TV director before retiring to write full time. I am also a devoted white baiter. My first novel was rejected by many publishers until a group of women formed Spiral Collective in order to publish it. The book won the New Zealand Book Award for fiction, the Mobil Pegasus Prize as well as the Booker Prize. Who am I? And what was the title of the book?

333. When I left school I trained as a jockey. I spent ten years living in the Greek Islands. When I returned to Australia I moved into radio. I was one of the early members of the *Coming Out Show* team. I presented First Edition and later The Europeans. I am now a Commissioning Editor for Arts National on ABC Radio. Who am I?

334. I was thrown out of the convent I attended in Townsville on my fourteenth birthday. A long-time activist for Aboriginal causes in Australia I was part of the Aboriginal Embassy that stood on the lawns of Parliament House for seven months in 1972. In the 80s I attended Harvard University where I received my doctorate. I am the author of a number of books including one I wrote with MumShirl. I have also written *Love Poems and Other Revolutionary Actions* and most recently *Black Majority*. Who am I?

335. Elsie Roughsey, who wrote *An Aboriginal Mother Tells of the Old and the New*, a book about her life on Mornington Island in the Torres Strait, is also known by another name. What is it?

336. I was born in New Zealand and I am famous around the world for my recitals of Mozart, opera and popular songs. Who am I?

337. I was born in Edinburgh in 1928. I studied music in Paris with Nadia Boulanger. I have worked as a conductor and have written opera, including *The Voice of Ariadne* (1973) as well as works for flute, *Orfeo* (1975) and dance. Who am I?

338. I was born in Canada, on Vancouver Island, in 1871. The Nootka people called me Klee Wyck, Laughing One. I painted many villages and totem poles in places such as Queen Charlotte Islands. My paintings were not recognized or appreciated until I was in my sixties. I am now one of Canada's best known artists and I am recognized for developing a distinctive Canadian style. Who am I?

339. Who co-founded The Hogarth Press in 1917?

340. Which story by Charlotte Perkins Gilman written in 1892 and based on her own life tells of a young mother driven mad and con-fined in a room by her doctor / husband?

341. Which of Christina Stead's novels, although set in 1930s Baltimore and Annapolis, actually draws on her childhood memories of Sydney?

342. Who showed up the publishing and literary world's treatment of new writers by using the pseudonym Jane Somers for her book *The Diary of a Good Neighbour*?

343. *The Wide Sargasso Sea* by Jean Rhys is based on the story of the mad wife in which Brontë novel?

344. Over the past few years there has been a campaign to preserve May Gibbs' Sydney home. The house is known as . . . ?

345. Name the author and the title of the novel about love, junkies and communal living that caused a stir when it was first published in Australia in 1977.

346. What do Jane, Julie, Gina and Alice have in common?

347. What is inscribed on the gold medallion that Barb gives to Brenda in Lisa Alther's *Other Women*?

348. Name three of the roles reconciled by Morgan Rose in *Mothers and Lovers* by Elizabeth Wood.

349. Who uttered the immortal words: 'My weight is always perfect for my height which varies.'?

350. And who created both the words and the character?

351. Who was Helen Keller's teacher?

352. A book in the New Testament – Acts – tells of a woman called Lydia who was a business woman in the rag trade. What commodity did she buy and sell?

353. In the novel *Pride and Prejudice* Lydia married Mr Wickham, and Elizabeth married Mr Darcy. Whom did Jane marry?

354. Colette writes of a 'sapphic poet' in *The Pure and the Impure*. To whom is she referring?

355. Who wrote the poem 'Before the flowers of friendship faded friendship faded'?

356. What is the name of Sally Morgan's grandmother in *My Place*?

357. What other artform, in addition to writing, does Sally Morgan work in?

358. I was born in Russia in 1885 and in 1913 I invented pasted cut-outs as a design technique, one which Henri Matisse was to use towards the end of his career. My designs influenced Paul Klee and my designs with stripes predated the American painters use of them by some forty years. By 1925 I was designing clothes that could still be worn today and be regarded as avant garde. The fabrics I designed were worn by Gloria Swanson and Nancy Cunard and the designs influenced the direction of modern clothing. I also designed sets and costumes for the theatre, film and ballet. In 1975 I designed a poster for UNESCO on the occasion of International Women's Year. I died in 1979 aged ninety-four. Who am I?

359. Tasma is the pseudonym of what Australian writer?

360. Who wrote the long poem *Goblin Market*?

361. What is the title of Edith Bagnold's famous book about a horse?

362. A popular English writer who writes both fiction and philosophy, what is her name?

363. What do Elizabeth Evatt, Deirdre O'Connor and Sally Thomas have in common?

364. The Congregationalist Church (now part of the Uniting Church) was the first church in Australia to ordain a woman, Winifred Kiek. In which year was she ordained?

365. Who launched her first and much-awaited book *Through My Eyes* in 1991?

366. H. D. are the initials of which American writer?

367. Who wrote *The Autobiography of Alice B. Toklas?*

368. I was born Tamara Gorska in Warsaw in 1898. Described in 1923 as the best of the Art Deco painters, my work combines strength and sensuality. I divorced my first husband, Tadeuz in 1928 and married a Hungarian Baron, Raoul Kuffner. I lived in Paris, Hollywood and New York and decorated the apartments of my friends including Helena Rubinstein's sister, Muzka Bernard. Many of my paintings are of women, including *Les Jeunes Filles* (1928) and a self portrait called *Auto-Portrait (Tamara in Green Bugatti)* (1925). By what name am I known?

369. I am the author of *One Writer's Beginnings*. I lived in Mississippi in the 1930s amongst rural blacks about whom I wrote and whom I photographed. What is my name?

370. In 1981 the life of a !Kung woman was published in which she says: 'There isn't a child whose birth is painless. It hurts like a terrible sickness.' What is her name?

371. I was born in Nigeria where I still live. My Ibu foremothers handed down a tradition of great strength to me. I am one of the best known African writers and the author of *Ifuru* and the long poem *Cassava Song and Rice Song* which deals with the politics of agriculture in third world nations. My press, Tana Press was the first independent women's press in Africa. Who am I?

238. 60–80%.

239. Thirteen.

240. Flora Tristan. Highgate Cemetery, London (next to Marx).

241. Judy Garland (1922–1969).

242. Mary Pickford.

243. Gloria Swanson.

244. Wallis Simpson, Duchess of Windsor.

245. Francesca Miles, independent feminist detective, in Melissa Chan's novel, *Too Rich.*

246. Elizabeth Taylor, in 1964.

247. By the guillotine.

248. Mary Shelley.

249. Tuberculosis.

250. Maria.

251. She took poison at age forty–two.

252. Martina Navratilova.

253. Babe Didrickson.

254. Mother-in-law.

255. Her mother.

256. Louisa Briggs.

257. Hyllus Maris.

258. Writer.

259. Bessie.

260. Forty-two minutes!

261. Sixty-seven.

262. Cécile Chaminade.

263. Yoko Ono.

264. Piaf.

265. Phranc.

266. Elisabeth Schwarzkopf.

267. Clara Schumann.

268. Fanny Mendelssohn.

269. Menolly.

270. Margaret Mitchell.

271. *Letters to my Daughter.*

272. Maud Sulter.

273. Miles Franklin.

274. Dymphna Cusack.

275. Margaret Catchpole (1762–1819).

276. Anne Bradstreet.

277. Victoria Woodhull, nominated by the Equal Rights Party in 1872.

278. Victoria Woodhull and Tennessee Claflin.

279. Mae West (1892–1980).

280. Lady Bird Johnson.

281. Marie Antoinette.

282. Rosa Luxemburg.

283. United Nations General Assembly.

284. *Contagious Diseases Acts.*

285. 1902. She was not admitted to practise as a barrister of the Supreme Court of New South Wales until 1921. After fighting each year subsequent to her graduation for the passage of the *Women's Legal Status Act* to enable her to go into practice.

The Act was passed in 1918.
Then, in order to comply with
the Barristers' Admission Rules,
shehad to be registered as a
student-at-law for two years.

286. Bea Miles.

287. Gertrude Jekyll.

288. Jo Spence.

289. Dorothea Lange.

290. Frida Kahlo and Tina
Modotti.

291. Julia Margaret Cameron.

292. Diane Arbus.

293. Lesbian (her lover was
Nesta Obermer, the painting is
reproduced on the Virago edition
of Radclyffe Hall's, *The Well of
Loneliness*).

294. Vera Brittain (1896–1970).
Friend and lover.

295. Virginia Woolf / Vita
Sackville-West / Violet Trefusis.

296. Vita Sackville-West.

297. Vanessa Bell.

298. Valentine Ackland.

299. Isabel Miller.

300. *The Ladies' Almanac.*

301. Radclyffe Hall.

302. Sarah Ponsonby.

303. Margaret Ponsonby.

304. Cow.

305. Suniti Namjoshi.

306. Gillian Hanscombe.

307. Lucrezia Borgia
(1480–1519).

308. Trotula.

309. Beguinages.

310. French.

311. Penelope.

312. Teresa of Avila (1515–1582).

313. Aphra Behn (1640–1689).

314. Hadewijch (Hadewych).

315. The Three Marias.

316. Remedios Varo.

317. Opera.

318. Dorothea MacKellar.

319. Oodgeroo Noonuccal
(formerly Kath Walker).

320. *Coonardoo.*

321. Charmian Clift.

322. Elizabeth Jolley.

323. Doris Lessing.

324. Karen Blixen; Ethel
Florence Robertson.

325. Barbara Vine.

326. P. D. James.

327. Amandine Aurore Lucie
Dupin (named at birth) Baronne
Dudevant (changed to in later
life).

328. Alice James.

329. *The Women's Room* by
Marilyn French.

330.

Lola Blau	Robyn Archer
Sybylla Melvyn	Miles Franklin
Mrs Ramsay	Virginia Woolf
Louie Pollitt	Christina Stead
Kezia	Katherine Mansfield
Evelina	Fanny Burney
Miss Peabody	Elizabeth Jolley
Fadette	George Sand
Snugglepot	May Gibbs
Maggie Tulliver	George Eliot
Squeaker's mate	Barbara Baynton
Emma	Jane Austen

331. *To the Is-Land / The Envoy from Mirror City.*

332. Keri Hulme, for ner novel, *the bone people.*

333. Julie Copeland.

334. Roberta Sykes.

335. Labumore.

336. Kiri Te Kanawa.

337. Thea Musgrave.

338. Emily Carr.

339. Virginia Woolf.

340. *The Yellow Wallpaper.*

341. *The Man Who Loved Children.*

342. Doris Lessing.

343. *Jane Eyre.*

344. Nutcote.

345. Helen Garner / *Monkey Grip.*

346. Their mother, Joanna May in Fay Weldon's novel.

347. *Plus que hier, moins que demain* / More than yesterday, less than tomorrow.

348. Head girl, hockey star, bush nurse, rebel, actress, feminist, wife, lesbian and mother.

349. Sylvia.

350. Nicole Hollander.

351. Anne Sullivan.

352. Purple cloth.

353. Mr Bingley.

354. Renée Vivien.

355. Gertrude Stein.

356. Daisy Corunna.

357. Painting / Prints.

358. Sonia Delauney.

359. Jessie Couvreur.

360. Christina Rosetti.

361. *National Velvet.*

362. Iris Murdoch.

363. Each was the first woman appointed to head a Court / Tribunal in Australia. Justice Elizabeth Evatt was the first Chief Judge of the Family Court of Australia, and the first woman Chief Judge of that court. Justice Deirdre O'Connor was the first woman appointed as President of the (Federal) Administrative Appeals Tribunal. Sally Thomas, C. M is Chief Magistrate of the Northern Territory Magistrates' Court, and the first woman ever appointed to head a Magistrates Court in Australia.

364. 1927.

365. Lindy Chamberlain.

366. Hilda Doolittle.

367. Gertrude Stein.

368. Tamara de Lempicka.

369. Eudora Welty.

370. Nisa (from the *Life and Words of a !Kung Woman*).

371. Flora Nwapa.

Time and Place

372. Before Everest was renamed after a Western man (Sir George Everest) the traditional name was Chomo-Lung Ma. What is the meaning of this name?

373. Name the place or culture of origin of the following goddesses:

Blodeuwedd	Isis
Nastséestsan	Aphrodite
Kunapipi	Kuanyin
Oya	Brigit
Chicomecoatl	Sarasvati
Freya	Pele
Harity	Mokosh

374. Hatshepsut said: 'My command stands firm like the mountains and the sun's disk shines and spreads rays over the titulary of my august person, and my falcon rises high above the kingly banner unto all eternity.' Which country did she rule?

375. What is the name of the mountaineer who wrote the popular book *Clouds from Both Sides* and who died in 1986 on the mountain, K2, that she had just successfully climbed?

376. Who am I? I was born in 1831 in Yorkshire, England. I came from a staid church family which I didn't leave until I was in my forties. Once I left, however, I really left, travelling all over the world and writing about my adventures with a lively and witty hand. I travelled to the Rocky Mountains, Japan, Korea, Hawaii and many other places.

377. In which century did Lady Ho of China write the following: 'When a pair of magpies fly together / They do not envy the pair of phoenixes.'?

378. Where does the band, 'The Flying Lesbians' come from?

379. From where do Anne McCaffrey's Dragonriders originate?

380. From which culture did the poet, Macuilxochitl (1435–1499) come?

381. Who invented Kabuki theatre?

382. *The Book of the City of Ladies* was written by Christine de Pisan in what century?

383. In which country did Khosrovidoukht Koghtnatsi (died 737) and Nahabed Kouchak (15th century) live?

384. Lal Ded, 16th-century poet from the Indian subcontinent, wrote in which language?

385. Which queen of England said: 'Much suspected of me, / Nothing proved can be.'?

386. Where were the following lines by Lady Jane Grey written: 'Think not, O mortal, vainly gay, / That thou from human woes art free; / The bitter cup I drink today, / Tomorrow may be drunk by thee.'?

387. Where was Caterina Sforza (1462–1509) when she wrote: 'Could I write all, the world would turn to stone.'?

388. In what century did Jezebel say : '. . . arise, and eat bread, and let thine heart be merry. . .'? (Kings, 21:7)

389. The Olgas in Central Australia were named after the Grand Duchess Olga Constantinova of which country?

390. What's so special about Charlotte Perkins Gilman's *Herland?*

391. Amazon Acres, Herland and The Valley in New South Wales are collectively known as . . . ?

392. From which modern-day countries did the ancient Thermadontines or Amazons come?

393. Of which ancient city were Khaizuran and Zubaidah queens?

394. Which famous ancient women were supposed to come from Libya?

395. In which language did Venmanipputi, write: 'my arms grow beautiful / in the coupling / and grow lean / as they come away. / What shall I make of this?' (Other poets who wrote in the same language between the first and tenth centuries AD include: Auvaiyar, Kaccipettu Nannakaiyar, Okkur Macatti and Andal. These poets are amongst the earliest writers on the Indian sub-continent.)

396. In which Indo-European language did the following poets write in the 500 year period from 650–1150 AD? Sila, Silabhlattarika, Vidya, Mahodahi, Vallana and Marula?

397. Queen Dahia-al Kahina in the 7th and 8th centuries resisted the advance of Islam and Christianity into Africa, including recapturing the ancient city of Carthage from the Arab general, Hassan-ben-Numan. Which modern-day country still bears the scars of her defensive action of laying the land waste so that food and water shortages would discourage the Arabs from returning?

398. In what year did Moroccan women gain the right to choose their own husbands?

399. Penthesilea was queen of what people?

400. What sisterhood did Brynhild belong to?

401. Melpomene, a Greek woman, ran the official marathon in four and a half hours, at the first modern Olympics. In what year was that?

402. When was the Olympic Marathon first opened to women?

403. Who rode from Ireland to India on a bicycle, and then wrote a book about it?

404. When was the first cycling event for women at the Olympics?

405. Who cycled down the Nile river from beginning to end?

406. Which country was ruled by the following women: Neith-hotep, Mer-Neith, Anchnesmerir, Nitocris, Sobeknofru, Ahotep, Ahmose-Nefetere, Hatshepsut, Mutemwia and Ta-wsret?

407. Gwerfyl Mechain (1460–1500) wrote: 'The moon in its robes of snow clouds / welcomes you / and your silver coins.' Where does she come from?

408. Which people worshipped the horse goddess Epona?

409. Described as two of Japan's legendary poets, Izumi Shikibu and Ono No Komachi wrote the following love poems: Izumi Shikibu: 'Why haven't I / thought of it before? / This body, / remembering yours, / is the keepsake you left' Ono No Komachi: 'My longing for you – / too strong to keep within bounds. / At least no one can blame

me / when I go to at night / along the road of dreams.' They wrote during the period when the emperors ruled from the city of Heian-kyo. Which modern-day city is this?

410 Sulpicia wrote: 'Drat my hateful birthday / to be spent in the boring old country.' and, 'Friends worry about me and are upset that somehow / I might tumble into bed with a nobody.' In what language did Sulpicia write?

411. Hildegard of Bingen was the head of what kind of institution?

412. Where are Ursula Le Guin's Tombs in the second of her Earthsea series?

413. Where does Persephone go in Autumn?

414. Who helped Theseus to find his way out of the labyrinth of Knossos?

415. Who wrote *Briefing for a Descent into Hell*?

416. From what country does Teresa of Avila come?

417. In which European language did the Jefimija (1348–1405) and Jevgenija (1353–1405) write?

418. Name the countries the following writers come from:

Nawal El Saadawi	Luisa Valenzuela
Clarice Lispector	Isabel Allende
Bessie Head	Maxine Hong Kingston
Christa Wolf	Marina Tsvetaeva
Janet Frame	Molly Keane

419. Where is Jeanette Winterson's novel, *Sexing the Cherry*, set?

420. Which arty and literary sisters lived at 46 Gordon Square in London?

421. Katherine Mansfield was born in which country?

422. What's at 84 Charing Cross Road, and who was interested?

423. What's at 68 Charing Cross Road, London today?

424. The Orient Express that Agatha Christie so immortalized began and finished its journey in which cities?

425. Which much celebrated and highly eccentric Victorian lady traveller and writer spent the last twenty-five years of her life in an old monastery, DarDjoun, in the foothills of Mount Lebanon?

426. In which year did British yachtswoman, Frances Clytie Rivett-Carnac win her event?

427. Maria Cunitz published a simplification of Keppler's tables of planetary motion entitled, *Urania propitia sive tabulae astronomicae mire faciles, vim hypothesium physicarum a Kepplero proditarum complexae, facillimo calculandi compendio sine ulla logarithmorum mentione phenomenis satisfacietes* in 1650. In which country did she live?

428. Dorothea Bocchi (Bucca) was appointed professor of medicine at the University of Bologna in which century?

429. Professor Enid Campbell was appointed the first female Professor of Law at what Australian university in 1967?

430. In which year did Marie Curie isolate a decigram of radium chloride, thereby enabling her to make the first determination of the atomic weight of radium, 225.93?

431. To which group of people do the following statistics apply: they are responsible for more than 50% of food production in developing countries; on the African continent they do 60–80% of all agricultural work, 50% of animal husbandry and 100% of all food processing; in industrialized countries they are paid one half to three quarters of what is considered the standard wage; they make up 90% of all refugee populations?

432. Match the following jumbled job ghettos for women in the 1980s with the country in which they occur:

doctors, road repair	UK
secretarial, office cleaning	Mexico
garment industry, electronics assembly	Nepal
lace working, cigarette production	China
Market trading, teaching	Uganda
road building	Brazil
charcoal selling	India
bank tellers	former USSR
weaving	USA
cotton and rice harvesting	Iran

433. What percentage of women are in the workforce in: Barbados, Romania, Mozambique, Sweden? (1975 percentages): 0–15%, 16–25%, 26–35%, 36–45%, over 45%?

434. What percentage of women are doing agricultural work in: Turkey, Mali, Madagascar? (1975 percentages): 0–20%, 21–40%, 41–60%, 61–80%, over 81%.

435. In which three Asian countries is sex tourism a major problem for women?

436. Feminist writer, Maria de Lurdes Pintassilgo coined the phrase 'pornography of power' to describe the basic connection between the propaganda of violence against women (pornography) and the practice of that violence. Which country does she come from?

437. Wivi Lönn (1872–1966) was the first woman architect in which country?

438. Which famous children's writer comes from Finland?

439. What does *Winnie the Witch* finally do about her cat?

440. Who created the language Láadan?

441. Which feminist science fiction writer created the world of 'Grass'?

442. Doris Lessing's first novel *The Grass is Singing* is set in which country?

443. When did Zimbabwe win the Women's Hockey Gold Medal?

444. Who won the Women's Hockey Gold Medal at the 1988 Olympics?

445. Who won the 1991 Netball World Title?

446. In what year did Jean Shrimpton shock Australians by wearing a mini-skirt to the Melbourne Cup?

447. Where did Joan Lindsay's picnic take place?

448. The novel *Come in Spinner* by Dymphna Cusack and Florence James is set in what city?

449. Where was Gladys Moncrieff born?

450. Who thought up the classic horror story 'The Lottery' as she returned home from a shopping expedition wheeling her baby in a pram?

451. The following Australian authors are associated with which jumbled places?

Daisy Bates	Blue Hills
Jean Devanny	Brindabella / Bin Bin
Colleen McCulloch	Gippsland
Eve Langley	Montsalvat
Gwen Meredith	Murray River
Miles Franklin	Perth / Western Australia
Nancy Cato	Norfolk Island
Betty Roland	Nullabor Plains
Aeneas Gunn	Queensland's cane fields
Elizabeth Jolley	The Never-Never

452. Where did Harry Lavender spend his life and commit his crimes?

453. What type of car does Katherine Forrest's detective Kate Delafield drive?

454. Where does V. I. Warshawski live and work? Who is her creatrix?

455. Which artist is responsible for inviting thirty-nine international guests to a dinner party?

456. Under which two paintings in the Metropolitan Museum of Art do the characters in Sandra Shotlander's play *Framework* meet?

457. Berenice Abbott's photographs are associated with which city?

458. Which great poet lived in Amherst, Massachusetts?

459. Patti Smith sings about searching on Redondo Beach? Where is Redondo Beach?

460. Leonora Carrington still lives in Mexico, though she also spends time in the US. She is both a painter and a writer. Her books include *The Hearing Trumpet* and *Down Below*, an account of her time in an asylum in Spain in 1942. She is one of many women who were active in the surrealist movement and both her paintings and writings draw on magical and occult traditions. In which country was she born?

461. In which country is Harriet Doerr's *Stones for Ibarra* set?

462. Sex tests were introduced for women at the Olympic Games held in Mexico. Which year was that?

463. Graciela Iturbide uses her sense of the bizarre and of the incongruous as a weapon. Women pose with iguanas on their heads or alongside a crocodile. From which country does Graciela Iturbide come?

464. From which country does Rigoberta Menchú come?

465. Who won the Nobel Peace Prize in 1992?

466. Fanny Burney, who lived into her nineties, wrote about age: 'How true it is, yet how consistent. . . that while we all desire to live long, we have all a horror of being old.' and, 'But an old woman. . . is a person who has no sense of decency; if once she takes to living, the devil himself can't get rid of her.' Which two centuries does her life span?

467. Jeanne Marie Roland (1754–1793), just before being guillotined, said: 'O liberty! what crimes are committed in thy name!' On what monument are these words inscribed?

468. When did Marie Antoinette say: 'I was a queen, and you took away my crown; a wife, and you killed my husband; a mother, and you deprived me of my children. My blood alone remains: take it, but do not make me suffer long.'?

469. Which country in the world has the only Feminist Party in government?

470. Who was elected Prime Minister of Norway in November 1990?

471. In what year did Indira Gandhi become Prime Minister of India?

472. Who dreamt of Manderley?

473. In 1982, German sociologist, Maria Mies wrote a book entitled *The Lace Makers of Naraspur*. In which country is Naraspur?

474. Which Burmese political figure won 80 per cent of the vote in elections held in 1989, and was then put under house arrest where she has remained since that time? In 1991 she won the Nobel Peace Prize.

475. Ambaphali wrote in the 4th century BC: 'Such was my body once. Now it is weary and tottering, the home of many ills, an old house with flaking plaster.' In what country did Ambaphali live?

476. In which language does Najma mostly write and sing?

477. Sophie Mgcina wrote the music for *Poppie Nongena*. This is a musical based on the life story of a woman from which country?

478. Ruth Neto was the elected Secretary-General of OMA in 1984. In which African country did OMA operate?

479. The novel *Ties of Blood* by Gillian Slovo is set in which country?

480. *The Dictionary of Composers and their Music* lists only seven women composers: Amy Mary Beach (1867–1944), Cécile Chaminade (1857–1944), Elisabeth Lutyens (1906–1983), Elizabeth Maconchy (1907–), Thea Musgrave (1928–), Priaulx Rainier (1903–) and Ethel Smyth (1858–1944). In which countries were these composers born?

481. From what country does the singer Mary Coughlan come?

482. Of which country was Maria Callas a citizen when she died?

483. Who was known as the 'Sibyl of the Rhine'?

484. From what country does Saint Bridget come?

485. Margery Kempe, the English mystic and writer, lived in which English county?

486. In which country was Eibhlín Dhubh Ní Chonaill born?

487. Which village was the home of the Brontë sisters?

488. Hannah Wakefield's Emma Victor was born in . . . . and moved to . . . . . to live and work.

489. Who is the woman at the helm?

490. In which language did Empress Nur Jahan write the following lines: 'Your love turned my body / into water.'?

491. 'You've made me all wet and slippery, / But no matter how hard you try / Nothing happens. So stop. / Go and make somebody else / Unsatisfied.' In what century did the Chinese poet, Huang O write these lines?

492. Esther said, 'Never let men mock at our ruin.' Of what country was Esther Queen?

493. In which Australian state was Aboriginal playwright, Eva Johnson's play, *Tjindarella*, first performed?

494. Who wrote 'Down City Streets' which appears on Archie Roach's *Charcoal Lane* cassette tape?

495. *Wandering Girl*, published by Magabala Books, an Aboriginal-run press, and written by Glenyse Ward describes events from Glenyse Ward's life that took place in which Australian state?

496. *Shame*, a film about rape, was made in which country?

497. How much money did Pat Lovell pay for an option to make a movie from the book, *Picnic at Hanging Rock*?

498. Which Pankhurst came to Australia?

499. Judo appears as a competitive sport for the first time for women in the Olympics in which year?

500. The first gold medal to be won by a woman in a swimming event was won by Fanny Durack in 1912. Which country was she representing?

501. In which year did Mary Decker and Zola Budd collide?

502. Anne of Green Gables' fame lived on which island?

503. In which century did the French poet, Louise Labé live?

504. Name five expatriate women writers who lived in Paris during the heady days between 1900 and 1940.

505. Who lived at 27 Rue de Fleurus in Paris?

506. Which famous poet lived on the Greek island of Lesbos?

507. Who was the first woman to attempt to fly around the world?

508. Ursula Le Guin wrote *The Word for World is . . . ?*

509. What does Gaia mean?

372. Goddess Mother of the Universe.

373. Blodeuwedd – Wales
Isis – Egypt
Nastséestsan – Navajo
Aphrodite – Greece
Kunapipi – Australia
Kuanyin – China
Oya – Yoruba
Brigit – Ireland
Chicomecoatl – Mexico
Sarasvati – India
Freya – Norway
Pele – Hawaii
Harity – Afghanistan
Mokosh – Russia

374. Egypt.

375. Julie Tullis.

376. Isabella Bird.

377. 300 BC.

378. Berlin.

379. Pern.

380. Aztec.

381. Japanese courtesans in the 16th century.

382. Fifteenth century.

383. Armenia.

384. Kashmiri.

385. Elizabeth I (1533–1603).

386. On a prison wall at the Tower of London in 1554.

387. In prison, in the Castel Sant'Angelo, Rome.

388. 9th century BC (874 BC–853 BC).

389. Russia.

390. It is an Amazon country run by and for women. It is considered a dangerous place for men to visit.

391. The Women's Land.

392. Iran and Iraq.

393. Baghdad, the capital of the Abbasid dynasty in the 8th and 9th centuries AD, or according to Islamic reckoning the 2nd century AH.

394. The Amazons. The Libyan Amazons rode on horseback and Strabo said of them 'there have been many generations of belligerent women in Libya'.

395. Classical Tamil.

396. Sanskrit.

397. Tunisia.

398. 1958.

399. The Amazons.

400. The Valkyries.

401. 1896.

402. 1984.

403. Dervla Murphy.

404. 1984.

405. Bettina Selby.

406. Ancient Egypt, also called Kemet.

407. Wales.

408. Celts/Welsh.

409. Kyoto

410. Latin.

411. Convent.

412. Atuan.

413. Hades/The Underworld.

414. Ariadne.

415. Doris Lessing.

416. Spain.

417. Serbian.

418. Nawal El Saadawi – Egypt
Luisa Valenzuela – Argentina
Clarice Lispector – Brazil
Isabel Allende – Chile
Bessie Head – Botswana
Maxine Hong Kingston – China
Christa Wolf – Germany
Marina Tsvetaeva – Russia
Janet Frame – New Zealand
Molly Keane – Ireland

419. The Thames River, London.

420. Vanessa and Virginia Stephen.

421. New Zealand.

422. An English bookshop (Messrs. Marks and Co.) / Miss Helene Hanff writes to the staff.

423. The feminist bookshop, Silver Moon Books.

424. London and Constantinople (Istanbul).

425. Lady Hester Stanhope.

426. 1908.

427. Germany.

428. Fourteenth century (1390), she held the post for forty years.

429. Monash University.

430. 1902.

431. Women (and children are included in the final 90% statistic).

432. doctors, road repair – former USSR
secretarial, office cleaning – UK
garment industry, electronics assembly – Mexico
lace working, cigarette production – India
Market trading, teaching – Brazil
road building – Nepal
charcoal selling – Uganda
bank tellers – USA
weaving – Iran
cotton and rice harvesting – China

433. All have over 45%.

434. All are over 81%, and this does not include subsistence agriculture which would involve many more women.

435. Thailand, Philippines, South Korea.

436. Portugal.

437. Finland.

438. Tove Jansson.

439. Instead of changing the cat different colours, she changes the house.

440. Suzette Haden Elgin in her novel, *Native Tongue*.

441. Sheri S. Tepper.

442. Rhodesia / Zimbabwe.

443. 1980.

444. Australia.

445. Australia.

446. 1964.

447. Hanging Rock.

448. Sydney.

449. Bundaberg, Queensland.

450. Shirley Jackson.

451. Daisy Bates – Nullabor Plains
Jean Devanny – Queensland's
     cane fields
Colleen McCulloch – Norfolk
     Island
Eve Langley – Gippsland
Gwen Meredith – Blue Hills
Miles Franklin – Brindabella /
     Bin Bin
Nancy Cato – Murray River
Betty Roland – Montsalvaat
Jeannie Gunn – The Never-
     Never
Elizabeth Jolley – Perth

452. Sydney – from the crime
novel with a woman sleuth by
Marele Day.

453. Plymouth.

454. Chicago, Sara Paretsky.

455. Judy Chicago.

456. 'Black Iris' by Georgia
O'Keefe and 'Gertrude Stein' by
Pablo Picasso.

457. New York.

458. Emily Dickinson.

459. Los Angeles.

460. England.

461. Mexico.

462. 1968.

463. Mexico.

464. Guatemala.

465. Rigoberta Menchú.

466. 18th and 19th centuries
(1752–1840).

467. The Statue of Liberty, New
York City.

468. 1793, on October 14 at the
revolutionary tribunal.

469. Iceland.

470. Gro Harlem Brundtland
(she was also Prime Minister in
1981 and 1986–89).

471. 1966.

472. The second Mrs Maxim de
Winter, in Daphne du Maurier's
novel, *Rebecca*.

473. India.

474. Aung San Suu Kyi.

475. India.

476. Urdu.

477. South Africa.

478. Angola. OMA =
Organization of Angolan Women.

479. South Africa.

480. USA, France, England,
England, Scotland, South Africa,
England.

481. Ireland.

482. Greece.

483. Hildegard of Bingen.

484. Ireland.

485. Norfolk.

486. Ireland (1743–1790).

487. Haworth.

488. USA / England.

489. Jeannine Talley – sailor.

490. Persian.

491. 16th century (during the
Ming Dynasty).

492. Persia. (Esther, 4: 17).

493. In South Australia at the Aboriginal Women's Arts Festival in 1984.

494. Ruby Hunter.

495. Western Australia.

496. Australia.

497. $100, in 1972.

498. Adele.

499. 1992.

500. Australia.

501. 1984 in the 3000 m race.

502. Prince Edward Island.

503. Sixteenth century (c.1524–1566).

504. Djuna Barnes / Natalie Barney / Kay Boyle / Colette / Nancy Cunard / H. D. / Janet Flanner / Mina Loy / Jean Rhys / Solita Solano / Gertrude Stein / Alice B. Toklas / Renée Vivien.

505. Gertrude Stein and Alice B. Toklas.

506. Sappho.

507. Amelia Earhart.

508. *Forest.*

509. Earth – originally from Greek.

Ideology

510. The author of *Through My Eyes*, published in 1981, says of the 'certificate of exemption' which she was granted in 1957 and which meant she was exempt from the restrictions imposed by the Aborigines Welfare Board that: 'I had to have this Certificate of Exemption. I had to be recommended to have it. I had to have it to go to any place from which an Aboriginal was banned, to take government jobs, and to leave the reserve. I could never work this out, in spite of my fight for rights. I had to have this piece of paper, like a passport, to give me rights in my own land; to be a citizen of Australia – my own country.' What was her name?

511. Why was Amalie Noether's appointment as a mathematician ended at Göttingen in 1933?

512. For which team did Hélène Mayer, fencing champion and known to be half Jewish, compete in 1936?

513. I am known as Germany's most prominent radical feminist of the 19th century. I never understood why men thought they were superior to women and wrote many irreverent treatises to put them in their place, especially the 'learned' ones. Friedrich Nietzsche is one of those whose anti-feminism I poked fun at in my book, *Die Antifeministen*. I was also the first woman to demand the vote for women in 1873 (which was called premature) and unrestrained access to any profession (especially medicine, law and natural science). I sometimes despaired at other women's liberalism and in 1902, at the age of sixtynine, I wrote: 'More pride, you women! How is it possible that you do not rebel against the contempt with which you are met . . . more pride, you women! The proud person may arouse disdain but not contempt. It is only on those who submit to the yoke that the would-be masters can put their foot.' What is my name?

514. Which Black American activist said: 'Den dat little man in black dar (a clergyman in the audience), he say women can't have as much rights as men, 'cause Christ wan't a woman! . . . Whar did your Christ come from? From God and a woman! Man had notin' to do wid Him'?

515. Commanded by her king to write him a poem, this Indian poet writing in the Kanada language wrote: 'Wasn't your mother a woman?

/ Who took care of you in your house, / a man? / Idiots! / Why do you vomit insults, screaming / 'woman, woman!' / What special virtue is there in a son / or perdition in a daughter? / Here and in the other world / happiness / comes to a person, not a gender. / A crude man is nothing, / A noble daughter is blessed forever.' What is the poet's name?

516. Who said: 'A quarrel between women is a victory for patriarchy?'

517. Who was the then little-known writer who wrote the following in a book published in 1936: '. . . there is too much fathering going on just now and there is no doubt about it fathers are depressing. Everyone nowadays is a father, there is Father Mussolini, and Father Hitler and Father Roosevelt and Father Stalin – and there are ever so many more ready to be one. Fathers are depressing, England is the only country now that has not got one and they are more cheerful there than anywhere.'

518. What issues does Eva Johnson write about in her three-monologue play, *What Do They Call Me?*

519. Bessy Cameron of the Nyungar people in Western Australia was well known as an accomplished pianist. She was appointed as a teacher of Aboriginal people at Lake Tyers, but her work was closely scrutinized. Due to the forces of racism Bessy was sacked and reinstated several times, as well as being forced to move off land by the *Half-Caste Act* in 1886. By the end of her life she was fighting again on behalf of her children and her children's children. For what end was she fighting?

520. Her work was described, during Hitler's reign, as degenerate. And yet her drawings, etchings, woodcuts, lithographs and sculptures done during World War I are amongst the most powerful anti-war art ever produced. She expressed through her work the plight of the oppressed, the causes of peace and social justice, the joys and sorrows of motherhood, and the misery of death. What is her name?

521. I am a Maori filmmaker and my documentaries, *Bastion Point* and *Patu* have won prizes in International Film Festivals. I was the first to film current events from a Maori perspective. I said: 'I think you can use tradition and culture as a form of oppression, or you can use it to progress by extending the barriers. How the hell are we expected to make any kind of progress economically, socially or politically if we continue to sit nicely with our hands folded and our mouths shut. What is my name?

522. Who said: '. . . rape . . . is nothing more or less than a conscious process of intimidation by which all men keep all women in a state of fear.'?

523. What happens once every ten minutes in Mexico City and once every six minutes in the US?

524. What rape law do Japan, Nigeria, Switzerland, Netherlands, India and Finland have in common?

525. What is involved in infibulation?

526. What is *sati* (suttee)?

527. In what year in Iran was the 'protective' overgarment, the *chador* made illegal?

528. In what year was the *chador* once again made compulsory?

529. In 1983 what happened to the following women in Iran: Iran's first woman physicist, a concert pianist, the former personnel director for Iran Television, a nurse and students?

530. Which Black American political activist, falsely jailed for her politics wrote: 'The master subjected her to the most elemental form of terrorism distinctly suited to the female: rape.'?

531. Which Australian feminist theorist wrote: 'Women have very little idea of how much men hate them.'?

532. What does a misogynist hate?

533. Who said: '"Hero" is the surprising word that men employ when they speak of Jack the Ripper'?

534. Ida Wells-Barnett wrote articles for a Memphis newspaper in the 19th century protesting what kind of racist action?

535. The British *Contagious Diseases Acts* of 1864, 1866 and 1869 were directed at which group of women?

536. In which European country is it still illegal to have an abortion?

537. Who said: 'If men could get pregnant, abortion would be a sacrament.'?

538. Gloria Steinem wrote the following in which book: 'So what would happen if suddenly, magically, men could menstruate and women could not? . . . Men would brag about how long and how much . . . Gifts, religious ceremonies, family dinners, and stag parties would mark the day . . . Doctors would research little about heart attacks . . . but everything about cramps . . . Sanitary supplies would be federally funded and free.'?

539. The term Revolutionary Feminists was born at the London Women's Liberation Movement Conference in 1977 with a paper called 'The Need for Revolutionary Feminism'. It grew out of Radical Feminism and Lesbian Feminism and by 1978 had grown into a vocal strand of the WLM who later founded WAVAW (Women Against Violence Against Women). Who coined the term?

540. Who framed the Minnesota *Antipornography Civil Rights Ordinances* which defined pornography as a civil rights issue for women?

541. What do healing, midwifery, impotent men, milkless cows, knowledge of botanical cures, wealth in a woman have in common?

542. What natural skin markings counted as 'witch's marks'?

543. 'Erica Huggins; Frances Carter; Rose Smith; Loretta Luckes; Margaret Hudgins; Maud Frances — 6 sisters in prison; 3 sisters pregnant; 2 sisters almost in labor. All have been falsely accused of conspiracy and murder. None have been tried or found guilty. All 6 are black.' To which Black organization did they belong?

544. The above statement was published in WITCH in November 1969. What does WITCH stand for?

545. I lived in the USA from 1826 to 1898 and encouraged women to be disloyal to the laws of the fathers. My major work was *Woman, Church and State* (1893) in which I condemn the church as 'The most stupendous system of organized robbery and it is woman that is being robbed, thereby . . . not only taking her self-respect but all rights of person; the fruits of her own industry, her opportunities of education, the exercise of her judgement, her own conscience, her own will.' I was too radical for many of my sisters and have largely been written out of history. Were it not for contemporary feminists such as Mary Daly and Sally Roesch Wagner who have republished my book, I might not been known at all. Who am I?

546. Which country was the first to grant the vote to women without any restriction on class or race?

547. I was the first President of the Woman's (Federal) Political Association in Australia and the first woman candidate in the British Empire
ever to stand for Parliament (the Senate) in 1903. My candidacy was
definitely feminist and I directed my campaign at women. I got 51,497
votes which even my opponents recognized as a considerable triumph
for anybody – and especially a woman – on a non-party ticket. I stood
four more times as an independent both for the Senate and Parliament,
but was never successful. Today, my contribution to the first years of
the nation's formation is often forgotten: the boys would have to look
at the part they played in keeping me out of power which does not
portray them in a flattering light. What is my name?

548. Who wrote *March of the Women*, a stirring suffragist orchestral
work?

549. Place the following jumbled countries and dates in the order in
which women achieved the right to vote without any property, class
or race restrictions.

New Zealand	1920	Switzerland	????
Australia	1956	USA	1915
UK	1965	Germany	1944
France	1991	Russia	1928
Finland	1893	Egypt	1979
Afghanistan	1945	Canada	1947
South Africa	1914	Japan	1918
Argentina	1906		

550. For what end did women in Britain do the following acts: pour
acid on golf greens; chain themselves to iron railings; burn railway
stations; attack government figures and go on hunger strike?

551. 'In education, in marriage, in religion, in everything, disappointment is the lot of women. It shall be the business of my life to
deepen this disappointment in every woman's heart until she bows
to it no longer.' For what right was Lucy Stone struggling when she
wrote this in 1855?

552. How much longer did women in the United States have to wait?

553. When men could claim any payment made to their writing
wives, one woman wrote a denunciation of her husband's despotism
and published it under the title, 'Let Him Claim Copyright to This'.
Who was she?

554. Complete the sentence that Lucretia Mott wrote in 1849: 'The

legal theory is, that   marriage makes the husband and wife one person, and that person is . . . ?'

555. Who said: 'Those comfortably padded lunatic asylums which are known, euphemistically, as the stately homes of England.'?

556. Who organized the International Women's Conference Against the War in 1915 against much political opposition?

557. In Sri Lanka in 1973 the prior statistic of women as 26% of the labour force rose steeply to 44.9%. What caused this sudden rise?

558. I had an enormous international reputation at the turn of the last century and my most famous book, *Women and Economics* (1898) was translated into seven languages. From 1909 to 1916 I edited and wrote for *The Forerunner*, a monthly US magazine dealing with topics from venereal disease to noise pollution with an overall focus on the rights of women and socialism. Throughout my life I had a passionate friendship with Grace Channing. Today I am mostly remembered for the description of my descent into madness as a new mother, *The Yellow Wallpaper*, following, but finally resisting Dr. Mitchell's 'Rest Cure' and resuming work which saved my life. Who am I?

559. Which New Zealand economist, writer and ex-politician has written of women's exclusion from the economics of capitalism and communism? What is the telling title of her book?

560. My slogan was 'Equal pay, equal status and equal opportunity' and I fought for this for over fifty years. I worked in many areas of union activity including the Federated Unions in Australia in 1919–1920. I wrote several influential articles including 'The Basic Wage Betrayal' in the early 20s, 'The Trade Union Women' in 1928 and 'Are Women Taking Men's Jobs?' in 1935. I proposed maternity and child allowances as a basic right for Australian women in the 20s. I established the Unemployed Girls Relief Movement during the Depression. I died at the age of eighty-nine in poverty in St Kilda. Who am I?

561. Who said: 'The definition of women's work is shitwork.'?

562. Who am I? I was born in 1858 and died in 1943. My husband and I were socialists. I was one of the founding members of the Fabian Society and the London School of Economics. I published a great deal of work focusing on labour and capital, as well as my diaries. Virginia Woolf didn't like me at all. My name is . . . ?

563. What did the film *For Love or Money* deal with?

564. Who said marriage was legal prostitution, but because prostitutes had more control over their time and payments they got a better deal than wives?

565. Of which people was Fredegund queen?

566. Who was the most famous member of the 'Gang of Four' in China?

567. Who became the first Australian woman premier?

568. Which recently deposed leader said the following: 'One of the things being in politics has taught me is that men are not a reasoned or reasoning sex.' ?

569. Who became the Premier of Israel in 1969?

570. Renée de France (1510–1575) said: 'Had I a beard I would have been the King of France.' Why couldn't she be Queen of France?

571. To which torturers did Maria Cazalla say the following: 'Why do you need to torture me? I have told the truth and can say no more. ' and, 'You do this to a woman? I dread more the affront than the pain.'

572. Who taught Gandhi everything he knew about civil disobedience?

573. Born in Holland as Gertrude Zelle, she was later accused by the French government of aiding the Germans and executed. By what name was she best known?

574. Who was the first New Zealand woman to be Minister of Finance?

575. Who was the first Australian woman to be appointed to the Cabinet?

576. How many women Supreme Court Judges are there in Australia in 1991?

577. What did the following headline on 1 January, 1975 herald?

$2 MILLION FOR THE SHEILAS – SURPRISINGLY IT'S NO JOKE.

578. Who was appointed as Special Adviser to Gough Whitlam on Women's Affairs in 1973?

579. Who resigned her membership of the US organization, Daughters of the Revolution when Black contralto, Marian Anderson was denied permission to perform at Constitution Hall?

580. Who wrote the first sociology textbook?

581. Who wrote: 'Alas, a woman that attempts the pen / Such an intruder on the rights of men.'?

582. Complete the famous graffiti: 'Boys will be boys, but girls will be . . . ?

583. Elizabeth Barrett Browning wrote the following in which poem: 'Men get opinions as boys learn to spell, / By reiteration chiefly . . .'?

584. Who said: '. . . a woman must have a room of her own if she is to write fiction.'?

585. Boosey and Hawkes, publishers of music, lost interest in 1945 when they discovered that the composer of Concerto for String Orchestra was a woman. Amongst other important works she composed music for poems by Judith Wright, called *Six Australian Songs* and an opera based on the life of Daisy Bates, *The Young Kabbarli*. She was largely responsible for securing the site for the present Victorian Arts Centre in Melbourne. What is her name?

586. The tenth century Japanese poet, Sei Shonagon, made lists of things she liked and things she disliked. The poetic form she invented still bears the name of her book. Here is an example that expresses sentiments of many modern-day women in numerous fields of work: 'Very Tiresome Things: When a poem of one's own, that one has allowed someone else to use as his, is singled out for praise.' What was the name of her book of poems?

587. Famous for her love letters, a medieval Frenchwoman wrote the following lines to her lover: 'Only tell me, if you can, why, since the retirement from the world which you yourself enjoined upon me, you have neglected me. Tell me, I say, or I will say what I think, and what is on everybody's lips. Ah! it was lust rather than love which attracted you to me. . .' Who wrote these lines?

588. Which Frenchwoman said: 'Genius has no sex!'?

589. In the first decade of this century my name was a household word in the USA. I was known as the 'Queen of Anarchists', 'Most Dangerous Woman in the World', 'Red Emma'. In 1917 I was deported to Russia. Today's feminists use one of my slogans on their T-Shirts, 'If I can't dance I don't want to be part of your revolution'. What is my name?

590. I aroused (and still do) powerful positive *and* negative emotional responses in other people. I was friends with Havelock Ellis, Eleanor Marx and Edward Carpenter, had lots of energy (some called it neurotic and 'frenetic manner of talking'), and always spoke my mind. Not for me any Victorian deference to men: I shouted them down, sneered at them, interrupted them and mocked them. I was born in South Africa to missionary parents, in 1855. I travelled widely and was one of the first internationally networking feminists. I lived my politics as well as wrote and spoke them and was passionately committed to 'new women' and the 'new life'. *The Story of An African Farm* is what most people know. The story of who I really was still needs to be written. What is my name?

591. Famous for her contribution to Marxist philosophy and to her critique of Fascism, who wrote the following: 'Wars and revolutions. . . have outlived all their ideological justifications. . . No cause is left but the most ancient of all, the one in fact, that from the beginning of our history has determined the very existence of politics, the cause of freedom versus tyranny.'?

592. Nguyen Thi Binh said in 1975: 'I was tortured [in the 1950s] by the Vietnamese, with the French directing, just as now it is with the Americans directing.' What government position did she hold?

593. Who wrote: 'And if the white man thought that Asians were a low, filthy nation, Asians could still smile – at least they were not Africans. And if the white man thought that Africans were a low, filthy nation, Africans in Southern Africa could still smile – at least they were not bushmen. They all have their monsters.'?

594. Which novelist from Ghana wrote the following: 'Awards / What / Dainty name to describe / This / Most merciless / Most formalised / Open, / Thorough, / Spy system of all time / For a few pennies now and a / Doctoral degree later, / Tell us about / Your people / Your history / Your mind'?

595. La-Neeta Harris was thirteen years old and at school in New York state when she wrote a manifesto called 'Black Women in Junior High School'. In what year did she write it?

596. Which US ex-Furies member now active in international feminism wrote: 'Feminism is an entire world view or gestalt, not just a laundry list of 'women's issues.'?

597. What political action did the following women all engage in:

Madame Tinubu of Nigeria; Nandi of the Zulu people; Kaipkire of the Herero people of South West Africa; and the female army that followed the Dahomian King, Behanzin Bowelle?

598. In what year did the first black model appear on the cover of *Vogue?*

599. Who wrote 'Goodbye to All That' first published in *Rat* in 1970 and then in *Sisterhood is Powerful.*

600. The first contemporary Women's Studies course is said to have taken place at Cornell University (USA) in 1968. But more than thirty years ago – 1934 – another woman in the US wrote a fifty-page pamphlet entitled 'A Changing Political Economy as it Affects Women' which was a detailed syllabus for a Women's Studies course and must be credited with being the first of its kind. In 1941 the same author wrote a forty-page feminist critique of the *Encyclopedia Britannica* (financed by the Encyclopedia itself). In 1946 she published *Woman as A Force in History.* In all her writing she asserted that women have always been a very real but highly neglected force in society. She never received the credit she was due. In 1977 Ann J. Lane republished some of her work in a source-book. What is her name?

601. What was the name of the US author who wrote a book on women's oppression particularly pertinent to married women in the early days of the second wave of contemporary feminism this century and entitled her first Chapter 'The problem that has no name'? When did she write the book and what was its title?

602. Who was the woman who said when she was asked in a discussion on sexist language what she thought about manholes: 'There should be more of them!'?

603. Complete the graffiti response to: If it [a car] were a lady, it would get its bottom pinched.

604. Who wrote in 1973: 'I never said I was a dyke even to a dyke because there wasn't a dyke in the land who thought she should be a dyke or even thought she was a dyke so how could we talk about it'?

605. Yoko Ono wrote the following in which book: 'I wonder why men can get serious at all. They have this delicate long thing hanging outside their bodies, which goes up and down by its own will . . . If I were a man I would always be laughing at myself.'?

606. Which important early work of feminist theory of the late 60s

analysed the work of Norman Mailer, Jean Genêt, D. H. Lawrence and Henry Miller?

607. 'Life in this society being, at best, an utter bore, and no aspect of society being at all relevant to women, there remains to civic-minded, responsible, thrill-seeking females only to overthrow the government, eliminate the money system, institute complete automation and destroy the male sex.' In which manifesto did this appear?

608. When did Sarah Moore Grimké write the following: 'I ask no favours for my sex. I surrender not our claim to equality. All I ask of our brethren is that they will will take their feet off our necks.'?

609. Maggie Kuhn (US) said: 'I enjoy my wrinkles and regard them as badges of distinction – I've worked hard for them.' Which organization did she found?

610. In Australia there is an annual 10/40 conference. What does 10/40 stand for?

611. What is the original meaning of the suffix –ix in words such as: obstetrix, creatrix, matrix, executrix?

612. When was the word 'Chairperson' first used in legislation in Australia?

613. What is the origin of the word 'trivia'?

614. Who wrote the famous words: 'One is not born, but rather becomes a woman.'?

615. 'I don't know what a feminist is but I know people call me that whenever I express an opinion that differentiates me from a doormat.' Who said this?

616. Which writer put forward this theory on the emergence of British women writers after the First World War? '. . . the men were dead, you see, and the women didn't marry so much because there was no one for them to marry, and so they had leisure, and, I think, in a good many cases money – because their blokes were dead, and all this would lead to writing wouldn't it, being single and having some money and having the time – having no men, you see.'

617. Name one of the three French feminists who Elizabeth Grosz writes about in *Sexual Subversions*.

618. Singer, Judy Small is known for her folk songs with a political bent. One of her songs, 'When the Party's Over', looks at Australian white oppression of Aborigines. Complete its refrain:

619. Which Australian poet, also known as an active conservationist, attacks Australia's history of crimes against the Aborigines and the land in her work?

620. Who wrote the classic feminist works: *The Second Sex* and *The First Sex*?

621. Who went way *Beyond God the Father*?

622. Which US woman writer started her feminist life as a married Mormon?

623. In which year was the first test-tube baby born?

624. What is the failure rate for women on IVF programs?

625. The Australian film *On Guard*, made by Sarah Gibson and Susan Lambert dealt with what feminist issue?

626. Queenslander, Jackie McKimmie was writer and director of a film about surrogacy. What is the film's name?

627. Who wrote *The Dialectic of Sex*?

628. What did African-American dancer, Janet Collins, refuse to do when offered a conditional position with the Ballet Russe de Monte Carlo?

629. The writing's on the wall – finish the graffiti: 'It begins with sinking into his arms and ends with . . . ?

630. Which feminist magazine, first published in 1972, changed its subtitle in 1977 from *A Women's Studies Journal* to *A Journal of Radical Feminist Thought*. The title of the journal has its roots in a chant the convict women invented. The journal is celebrating its twentieth anniversary in 1992.

631. The Australian journal *Scarlet Woman* focuses on what kind of feminist thought?

632. How many female Professors of Law had been appointed in Australia by August 1991?

633. What is the graffiti writer's response to: 'Renew his interest in carpentry?'

634. How were athletes and coaches sex tested after 440 BC to ensure women were kept out?

635. Why were women made to cover their hair in church?

636. What Australian organization uses the abbreviation WWWW?

637. Which Australian poet was taken to court by her ex-husband because of a poem?

638. Which book by Amanda Lohrey was banned?

639. Who wrote the following, and in which of her books? 'Women have served all these centuries as looking glasses, possessing the magic and delicious power of reflecting the figure of a man at twice its natural size.'

640. Who uttered the immortal words: 'Thank God for Dale Spender.' ?

641. In which years have women's organizations intervened in Basic Wage Cases, Equal Pay Cases, Minimum Wage Cases, and/or National Wage Cases before the Australian Industrial Relations Commission and its precursors?

510. Ella Simon (1902–1981).

511. Because she was Jewish.

512. Germany.

513. Hedwig Dohm (1933–1919).

514. Sojourner Truth (c. 1797–1883).

515. Honnamma (1665–1699).

516. Dale Spender.

517. Gertrude Stein in *Everyone's Autobiography.*

518. The kidnapping and separation of Aboriginal children from their mothers.

519. She was fighting to stop her children being taken, as she had been, to be brought up 'white'.

520. Käthe Kollwitz.

521. Merata Meta.

522. Susan Brownmiller, in *Against Our Will: Men, Women and Rape,* published in 1975.

523. A woman is raped.

524. Wife rape is not acknowledged as a crime.

525. Cutting of clitoris, labia minora and part of the labia majora. Most of the vaginal opening is then stitched together. Although most frequently practised in Africa and the Middle East, it also occurs in the West.

526. When a widowed Hindu woman, whether by physical force or peer pressure, burns to death on the pyre of her

husband. Although outlawed in India where the practice most frequently occurred, there are still reports of this happening.

527. 1936.

528. 1983.

529. They were executed by the Islamic Revolutionary Court.

530. Angela Davis in *The Black Scholar,* 1971.

531. Germaine Greer in *The Female Eunuch,* 1971.

532. Women.

533. Susan Brownmiller.

534. Lynching.

535. Prostitutes (in garrison towns prostitutes were required to subject themselves to compulsory physical examination and treatment for disease, while no such requirement was placed on their clients – men).

536. Eire (Republic of Ireland).

537. Florynce R. Kennedy (1916–).

538. *Outrageous Acts and Everyday Rebellions.*

539. Sheila Jeffreys.

540. Catharine MacKinnon and Andrea Dworkin.

541. All are cause for accusations of witchcraft.

542. A mole, wen, any part of the body that did not bleed when pricked (possibly caused by a build up of scar tissue), any

defined by the witch hunters), any puckering of skin.

543. The Black Panther Party.

544. Women's International Terrorist Conspiracy from Hell. WITCH formed in 1967.

545. Matilda Joslyn Gage (1826–1898).

546. NZ in 1893.

547. Vida Goldstein (1869–1949).

548. Ethel Smyth.

549.
New Zealand	1893
Australia	1902
Finland	1906
Germany	1914
Russia	1917
Canada	1918
USA	1920
UK	1928
France	1944
Japan	1945
Argentina	1947
Egypt	1956
Afghanistan	1965
Switzerland	1991
South Africa	????

550. The vote.

551. The right to vote.

552. The vote was achieved in 1920 – sixty-five years!

553. Caroline Norton.

554. The husband.

555. Virginia Woolf, from 'Lady Dorothy Nevill', *The Common Reader*, 1925.

556. Clara Zetkin.

557. Housewives were included for the first time as workers.

558. Charlotte Perkins Gilman (1860–1935).

559. Marilyn Waring, *Counting for Nothing*.

560. Muriel Heagney, 1885–1974.

561. Gloria Steinem in 1974.

562. Beatrice Webb.

563. The history of women and work in Australia.

564. Mary Wollstonecraft in *Vindication of the Rights of Women*, 1792.

565. The Frankish people; she died in 597 AD.

566. Jiang Qing (Chiang Ch'ing).

567. Carmen Lawrence.

568. Margaret Thatcher.

569. Golda Meir.

570. Salic law (derived from a 5th century Frankish code) prevented women from succeeding to the throne.

571. The Inquisition.

572. Christabel Pankhurst.

573. Mata Hari.

574. Ruth Richardson.

575. Susan Ryan.

576. One. Justice Jane Matthews.

577. The money was allocated by the Whitlam Government for the International Women's Year program.

578. Elizabeth Reid.

579. Eleanor Roosevelt, in 1939.

580. Harriet Martineau with *How*

to Observe; Morals and Manners, 1858.

581. Anne Finch, Countess of Winchelsea.

582. Women.

583. *Aurora Leigh*, Bk. VI, 1. 6, 1857.

584. Virginia Woolf.

585. Margaret Sutherland.

586. *Pillow Book.*

587. Héloïse.

588. Germaine de Staël (1766–1817).

589. Emma Goldman (1869–1940).

590. Olive Schreiner (1855–1920).

591. Hannah Arendt (1906–1975).

592. Foreign Minister (of the South Vietnamese Liberation Front).

593. Bessie Head in her novel, *Maru*, 1971.

594. Ama Ata Aidoo in her novel, *Our Sister Killjoy, or Reflections from a Black-eyed Squint.*

595. 1970.

596. Charlotte Bunch.

597. They all resisted the European slave trade.

598. 1987.

599. Robin Morgan.

600. Mary Ritter Baerd (1876–1958).

601. Betty Friedan, 1963, *The Feminine Mystique.*

602. Dale Spender.

603. 'If this lady was a car she'd run you down'?'

604. Jill Johnston in *Lesbian Nation.*

605. *Grapefruit*, published in 1970.

606. *Sexual Politics* by Kate Millet, published in 1969.

607. *SCUM Manifesto*, 1967–1968 by Valerie Solarnas.

608. 1837 in a letter to Mary S. Parker, President of the Boston Female Anti-Slavery Society.

609. Gray Panthers.

610. Women who are over forty years of age who have been members of the women's movement for ten or more years.

611. It indicated that the person was female – one can deduce from the prior existence of such words to their masculine counterpart (creator, for example) that these were originally roles undertaken by women.

612. 1984 – in the Law Reform Commission Act.

613. It refers to the three (tri-) ways (via) or crossroads sacred to goddesses such as Hecate Trevia. These were meeting places where people met to gossip and pass on information and news. Trivia is therefore important knowledge.

614. Simone de Beauvoir.

615. Rebecca West.

616. Ivy Compton-Burnett.

617. Julia Kristeva/Luce Irigaray/Michele Le Doeuff.

618. 40,000 years is not a Bi-Centenary.

619. Judith Wright.

620. Simone de Beauvoir, Elizabeth Gould Davis.

621. Mary Daly.

622. Sonia Johnson.

623. 1978, Louise Brown in England.

624. 90–95 per cent.

625. Reproductive technology.

626. *Waiting.*

627. Shulamith Firestone

628. She refused to wear white make-up to lighten her skin.

629. 'Your arms in the sink.'

630. *Refractory Girl.*

631. Socialist feminist.

632. Seven. Prof. Enid Campbell, Monash University; Prof. Alice Eh Soon Tay, University of Sydney; Prof. Maureen Brunt, Monash University; Prof. Marcia Neave, Adelaide University; Prof. Helen Gamble, Wollongong University; Prof. Cheryl Saunders, Melbourne University; Prof. Margaret Thornton, Department of Legal Studies, La Trobe University.

633. 'Saw his head off.'

634. They had to register naked.

635. Hair was magically associated with the spirit world and unbinding the hair could raise storms and control the spirit world. In order to prevent this

women were ordered by St Paul to cover their heads when praying or prophesying.

636. Women Who Want to be Women – an anti-feminist organization.

637. Dorothy Hewett.

638. *The Reading Group.*

639. Virginia Woolf in *A Room of One's Own.*

640. Jeanette Winterson.

641. 1949–50, *Basic Wage Case* – Australian Federation of Business and Professional Women (AFPBW) and National Council of Women (NCW).

1969, *National Wage Case/Equal Wage Case* – the Union of Australian Women (UAW) and the Australian Federation of Women Voters.

1972, *National Wage Case/Equal Pay Case* – NCW, UAW, and the Women's Liberation Movement.

1974, *Equal Pay Case/Minimum Wage Case* – UAW, NCW, Women's Electoral Lobby (WEL).

1983, *National Wage Case* – UAW, NCW, WEL.

1988, *National Wage Case* – National Pay Equity Coalition.

1990–91, *National Wage Case* – AFPBW.

Sport and Culture

642. What did the suffragettes dig up in relation to the golf-playing establishment which made men think it would be better to give women the vote?

643. Who is the sole woman to have won a gold medal in Golf?

644. What horse sport now associated with royalty was once played by Persian women?

645. Who said: 'The horse is just about the only one who doesn't know I'm royal.'?

646. In 396 BC the Spartan princess, Kyniska, became the first woman Olympic champion by winning which race?

647. Who became the world heptathlon champion in 1987?

648. Who was the 'Golden Girl' of Australian athletics?

649. At which sport did Heather McKay excel?

650. To 1991, how many times had Martina Navratilova won the Wimbledon Singles title?

651. Which Australian Aboriginal woman has won Wimbledon?

652. The invention of which vehicle was important in furthering the demands for 'bifurcated garments' for women in the late 19th century?

653. After which American feminist were bloomers named?

654. Which Roman born couturier was the first to feature padded shoulder (1931–32), zip fastenings, and synthetic fabrics?

655. Whose designs were dubbed 'post-Hiroshima' when they were displayed in 1983?

656. Who wrote the script for *Hiroshima, mon amour*?

657. Who directed *A Question of Silence* and *Broken Mirrors?*

658. Who directed *Dark Times?*

659. Who made the film, *Olympische Spiele* (*Triumph of Will*) about the Nazi Games in Berlin in 1936?

660. Which race did Debbie Flintoff win at the 1988 Olympics?

661. In which sport did Australia win the inaugural world champion-ship in 1965?

662. Who won the most Olympic Gold Medals of any Australian in a single Olympic Games?

663. Who is the only female competitor to win gold medals in the same event in three successive Olympic Games?

664. Who said:' People think of me as the incredible hulk.' ?

665. For which sport is Fatima Whitbread famous?

666. Who was the tallest and heaviest woman to be an Olympic champion?

667. Which countries entered women in their shooting teams in the 1964 Olympics?

668. Who is the youngest medalist of either sex in the shooting events?

669. Who is the youngest archery Olympic Champion?

670. Ilona Elek of Hungary competed in the fencing events in 1936 and 1948. How many wins did she have in the two Olympics?

671. Who sings the songs 'Lola' and 'Ich bin von Kopf bis Fuss auf Liebe eingestellt' in the film *The Blue Angel?*

672. What do Iva Smith, Memphis Minnie, Lil Johnson, St Louis Bessie, Bessie Smith and Billie Holiday have in common?

673. Who made 'Me and Bobby McGee' famous?

674. Who wants to drive in an open sportscar through the streets of Paris with the wind blowing her hair?

675. Match the following jumbled jazz musicians with their instrument:

Janice Robinson	vibes
Willene Barton	harp
Carla Bley	violin
Vi Redd	accordion
Corky Hale	tenor sax
June Rotenberg	trumpet
Dorothy Ashby	alto sax
Peggy Gilbert	ukulele
Bridget O'Flynn	keyboards
Audrey Hall Petroff	organ
Sarah McLawler	bass
Irma Young	drums
Doris Peavey	trombone
Betty Sattley Leeds	reeds
Ann Patterson	alto sax
Estelle Slavin	flute

676. Who won the first gold medal in the Standard Rifle event in 1984?

677. In 1902 a British woman, Madge Syers entered the world championships in an event supposedly only for men and was placed second. In which sport was this?

678. Ludmila Khvedosyuk Pinayeva has won three gold medals in which sport?

679. Who is the only competitor to score a 'perfect' score in gymnastics?

680. Who invented what is labeled as 'killer gymnastics'?

681. Who wrote 'Ode to a Gym Teacher'?

682. On which record by Joan Armatrading does the song 'Willow' appear?

683. 'Good evening. This is your Captain. / We are about to attempt a crash landing.' Who wrote and sings these lines?

684. Who wrote *Pack of Women*?

685. The musical *Pack of Women* centres around what game?

686. Which Australian directed *Fourteen's Good, Eighteen's Better, High Tide* and *My Brilliant Career*?

687. Who played Sybylla Melvyn in the film of Miles Franklin's novel, *My Brilliant Career*?

688. Who was the producer of *Eden's Lost* and *For Love Alone*?

689. 'Last night I heard the screaming / Loud voices behind the wall / Another sleepless night for me / It won't do no good to call / The police / Always come late / If they come at all' Who wrote and sings these lines?

690. In which collection of Sylvia Plath's poetry do the following lines appear: 'A living doll, everywhere you look. / It can sew, it can cook, / It can talk, talk, talk. / It works, there is nothing wrong with it. / You have a hole, it's a poultice. / You have an eye, it's an image. / My boy, it's your last resort. / Will you marry it, marry it, marry it'?

691. Which American opera singer said the following: 'The thing to do [for insomnia] is to get a opera score and read *that*. That will bore you to death.'?

692. Which opera singer is known by the title *La Stupenda*?

693. There are two famous Flower Duets for two female voices. In which operas do they occur?

694. What is the title of Sinéad O'Connor's first recording?

695. Patty, LaVerne and Maxine are sisters. By what name are they known on their recordings?

696. What was special about the 1984 100m freestyle?

697. Which sport had its debut at the Olympics in 1988 and had never been at the Olympics before, even as a demonstration?

698. Frances Clytie Rivett-Carnac was the first woman to win an event not restricted to women or mixed pairs in any sport. What did she win?

699. Who was the first mother to run an Olympic race?

700. What were Soviet runner Irina Nazarova and Soviet discus medalist, Elizabeta Bagriantseva famous for?

701. Who won the first women's marathon?

702. Which New Zealand leading middle-distance runner is an Olympic Gold Medallist, was also USA Runner of the Year in 1982, and won 108 out of 120 races?

703. Of the fourteen possible gold medals in track and field and swimming, how many did East Germany win in 1976?

704. What distinguishes the childhood of Wilma Rudolph, American sprinter, from other athletes?

705. Who was the first athlete to win the 200m and 400m race at a single Olympics?

706. Which famous swimmer said: 'I hated the easy assumption that girls had to be slower than boys.'

707. Who was the first Black woman to win an Olympic throwing event?

708. For what sport is Norwegian Grete Waitz famous?

709. Who is the only runner in the world to hold, simultaneously, the 5,000m, 10,000m, 15,000m, half-marathon and marathon world records?

710. Who was the first Black American to play tennis at the US Open (1950) and Wimbledon (1951)?

711. Who jumped seventeen fences when concussed?

712. What is so special about *Princess Smartypants*?

713. Who is Miss Fanshawe?

714. History is being made. The world champion is a woman. Who was this said of in 1986?

715. Who is the oldest-ever woman to compete in the Olympics?

716. 'Some say an army on horseback, / some an army on foot, / still others say a fleet of ships remains / the most beautiful sight in / this dark world; / but I say it is / the one you love.' Who wrote this?

717. Who wrote: 'An army of lovers shall not fail.'

718. *The Beverley Malibu* is to *Amateur City* and *Murder at the Night-wood Bar* as *A Captive in Time* is to . . . ?

719. What are the two things Kaz Cooke highly recommends for cheering yourself up?

720. *What Comes Naturally?*

721. Who is the tenth muse?

722. What did the Troubadour women Alais, Carenza and Iselda do together?

723. Which renaissance French poet wrote the following: 'Kiss me again, rekiss me, kiss me more, / give me your most consuming tasty one, / give me your sensual kiss, a savory one, / I'll give you back four burning at the core.'?

724. She is known for her collected letters, *Staying on Alone*, for typing and editing Gertrude Stein's manuscripts with whom she lived for nearly forty years, and for her cookbook. What is the name of her cookbook?

725. Who wrote the song from 1965 called 'White Rabbit' in which occur the lines: 'Remember what the doormouse said: / 'Feed your head. / Feed your head. / Feed your head.'?

726. Who wrote *for colored girls who have considered suicide/when the rainbow is enuf*?

727. I have lived in many countries including France, Italy, Greece, Egypt and India which I have written about in numerous books. My contribution to the field of cookery and wine has been recognized by awards in Britain and France including an OBE, an honorary doctorate of the University of Essex, a Fellow of the Royal Society of Literature and a CBE. My books include *Mediterranean Food, French Provincial Cooking* and *An Omelette and a Glass of Wine*. Who am I?

728. Which South Australian winemaker started Marienberg wines?

729. What famous Australian gardener promoted roadside conservation?

730. What is the name of Vita Sackville-West's country home and famous garden?

731. Which European ruler of the 18th century, known for her correspondence with Voltaire, was a leading patron of the arts and gardening?

732. What kind of garment is a frou-frou?

733. One of the first film producers in Australia, with husband Charles she worked on numerous films as assistant director, co-writer, associate producer, dialogue director, and once in an acting role. She co-produced *Jedda* and a cinema in Sydney bears their name. What is her name?

734. Alma de Groen wrote the script for the telefeature *Man of Letters*. Who wrote the novel?

735. Jessica Anderson and Thea Astley have won which prestigious Australian literary award more than once?

736. Who was the presenter of *The Big Gig*?

737. Who said: 'Where would we be without the movies?'

738. Eva Jessye was the Choral director for which famous Gershwin opera?

739. What new elements did Katherine Dunham introduce into modern dance in the 30s?

740. What is the characteristic of traditional Yoruba plaiting worn by the High Priestess of the River Goddess?

741. Which black South African singer made the record *Pata Pata*?

742. 'Sweet Honey in the Rock' are described as what kind of group?

743. Which Irish musician wrote the music for the BBC TV series, *The Celts*?

744. Who sings 'Hymn to Her'?

745. The photographers Lucia Moholy and Lotte Beese were associated with which art school in Weimar?

746. Jan Groover is known for what kind of photography?

747. Who are Somerville and Ross?

748. Natalia Goncharova worked with Sergei Diaghilev and Igor Stravinsksy in what kind of work?

749. The Alyawarre and Anmatyerre women from Utopia in Central Australia are particularly well known for what kind of art work?

750. What do Ethel Spowers, A. M. E. Bale, Clara Southern, Vida Lahey, Thea Proctor, Grace Cossington-Smith, Margaret Bevan and Dora Searle have in common?

751. WHEN RACISM & SEXISM ARE NO LONGER FASHIONABLE, WHAT WILL YOUR ART COLLECTION BE WORTH?

The art market won't bestow mega-buck prices on the work of a few white males forever. For the 17.7 million you just spent on a single Jasper Johns painting you could have bought at least one work by all these women and artists of color:

Bernice Abbott   Annie Albers   Sofonisba Anguisolla   Diane Arbus Vanessa Bell   Isabel Bishop   Rosa Bonheur   Elizabeth Bougereau Margaret Bourke-White   Romaine Brooks   Julia Margaret Cameron Emily Carr   Rosalba Carriera   Mary Cassatt Constance   Marie Charpentier   Imogen Cunningham   Sonia Delauney   Elaine de Kooning Lavinia Fontana Meta Warwick Fuller Artemesia Gentileschi Marguérite Gérard   Natalia Goncharova   Kate Greenaway   Barbara Hepworth   Eva Hesse   Hannah Hoch   Anna Huntingdon   May Howard Jackson   Frida Kahlo   Angelica Kauffmann   Hilma af Klimt Käthe Kollwitz   Lee Krasner   Dorothea Lange   Marie Laurencin Edmonia Lewis   Judith Leyster   Barbara Longhi   Dora Maar   Lee Miller Lisette Model   Paula Modersohn-Becker   Tina Modotti   Berthe Morisot Grandma Moses   Gabriele Münter   Alice Neel   Louise Nevelson Georgia O'Keefe   Meret Oppenheim   Sarah Peale   Ljubova Popova Olga Rosanova   Nellie Mae Rowe   Rachel Ruysch Kay Sage Augusta Savage   Vavara Stepenova   Florine Stettheimer   Sophie Taeuber-Arp Alma Thomas   Marietta Robusti Tintoretto   Suzanne Valadon Remedios Varo   Elizabeth Vigée Le Brun   Laura Wheeling Waring.

Which organization wrote the above manifesto?

752. Who created the Fairy Tree in the Fitzroy Gardens, Melbourne?

753. What Japanese poetic form is the following poem by Kawai? Chigetsu-Ni (1632–1736): 'Grasshoppers / Chirping in the sleeves / Of a scarecrow.'

754. American artist living in London, Mary Kelly documented the growth and development of her new-born son. It was produced between 1973 and 1979. What is the name of this work?

755. Ezra Pound in *The Pisan Cantos* mentions Yeats, Beardsley, Ford, William, Eliot, Joyce, Symonds, Hulme, Lewis, Hemingway and Antheil, but he does not mention D. Marsden, H. Monroe, H. Weaver, M. Moore, A. Lowell, M. Loy, S. Beach, H. Doolittle or D. Richardson.

What are the first names of those in the second group?

756. Who invented stream-of-consciousness writing in her novel, *Pilgrimage*?

757. What is the real name of the poet known as 'The Matchless Orinda'?

758. Who wrote the famous Scottish song to Charles Edward Stewart, (a.k.a. Bonnie Prince Charlie and The Young Pretender) that begins: 'O, Charlie is my darling, / My darling, my darling; / Charlie is my darling, / The young Chevalier.'?

759. In which novel did Jane Austen write: 'An annuity is a very serious business.'?

760. Which of the world's great letter writers and figure in 17th century French society and literary circles, made the following observation: 'Luck is always on the side of the big battalions.'

761. Amy Mary Beach made her debut in 1885 and she created a work called *The Chambered Nautilus*. In which art form did she work?

762. *The Jesse Tree* is a Masque written by Anne Ridler and first performed in 1970. Who wrote the music for the work?

763. Priaulx Rainier was born in South Africa and some of her music draws on Zulu rhythms and melodies. She studied with Nadia Boulanger briefly in 1939. She was a close friend of artist, Barbara Hepworth. Her work *The Bee Oracles* honoured which experimental English poet?

764. What is the name of the only woman Troubadour (Trobairitz) whose music has survived to the present day?

765. The Australian contemporary composer Ros Bandt has invented a percussion instrument called a flagone. What is this instrument made from?

766. Caroline Newcombe (1812–1874) and Anne Drysdale (1792–1853) were responsible for setting up what kind of business?

767. Name the two sequels to *Seven Little Australians*.

768. What is the name of the children's book Louisa Lawson wrote?

769. What is unusual about the character Nosy Alf in Joseph Furphy's Australian novel *Such is Life*?

770. In which of her books did Emma Goldman (1869–1940) write: 'As to the eradication of prostitution, nothing can accomplish that save a complete transvaluation of all accepted values – especially the moral ones – coupled with the abolition of industrial slavery.'?

771. Who wrote: 'If there is anything disagreeable going on men are always sure of getting out of it . . .'?

772. What domestic activity was Tillie Olsen writing about in the story that contains these lines: 'And when is there time to remember, to sift, to weigh, to estimate, to total?'

773. Which film star said: 'I always wear slacks because of the brambles and maybe the snakes. And see this basket? I keep everything in it. So I look ghastly do I? I don't care – so long as I'm comfortable?.

774. About whom was Dorothy Parker writing in this review: 'She runs the gamut of emotions from A to B.'?

775. Ann Ronell, songwriter, composer and orchestra conductor and the first woman to conduct and compose for film, is famous for her work with which American movie company that specializes in works for children?

776. Who said: 'Had I been a man I might have explored the Poles or climbed Mount Everest, but as it was I found spirit in the air. . .'?

777. Which US fiction writer, pacifist and anti-Vietnam activist wrote: 'I was a fantastic student until ten, and then my mind began to wander.'?

778. Who wrote *To Kill a Mockingbird*?

779. What was the title of Shirley MacLaine's autobiography published in 1970?

780. Who said: 'I don't want to make money. I just want to be wonderful.'?

781. In what way was Hungarian chess player, Judith Polgar, wonderful?

782. Who wrote: '. . . a woman is talking to death . . .'?

783. 'And I will speak less and less to you / And more and more in crazy gibberish you cannot understand: / witches' incantations, poetry, old women's mutterings . . .' Who wrote these lines?

784. Who searched for her mother's garden and found her own?

785. In which novel did Christina Stead write: '. . . the waste, the insane freaks of these money men, the cynicism and egotism of their life . . . I'll show that they are not brilliant, not romantic, not delightful, not intelligent.'?

786. Known for her ascerbic wit, she was a formidable critic for *The New Yorker* and other magazines. In 1922 she wrote: 'The affair between Margot Asquith and Margot Asquith will live as one of the prettiest love stories in all literature.'?

787. Who sang the hit song, 'I Am Woman'?

788. Which Australian singer and performer starred in the musical, *Piaf*? She has also produced the records, *Free Fall through Featherless Flight* and *Looking Backwards to Tomorrow*.

789. Kay Gardner, composer and accompanist to Alix Dobkin on *Lavender Jane Loves Women*, plays what instrument?

790. Who says: 'Ain't Life a Brook?'

791. What does Kathleen Battle sing?

792. Mitsuko Uchida is known for her inspired performances of which composer's work for piano?

793. German woodwind player, Sabine Meyer, plays what instrument?

794. Who wrote 'A rose is a rose is a rose'?

795. Peggy Guggenheim is associated as a patron with which art form?

796. A collaboration between a writer and an artist produced the book *Wahine Toa: Women of Maori Myth*. Who were the collaborators?

797. What is the name of the central character in Alice Walker's *The Color Purple*?

798. What is the English (original) title of Merlin Stone's book *When God Was a Woman*?

799. What is the subtitle of Sue Ingleton's *Almaniac*?

800. Who directed the film *Sweetie*?

801. What is the name of the only Australian magazine to review women's books?

802. What is the only national festival for writers held in Australia every two years? The festival promotes women's writing.

803. What are the two US magazines that review women's books called?

804. What is the name of the central female character in *Wuthering Heights?*

805. Madame Becl appears in which of Charlotte Brontë's novels?

806. Dorothy Sayers is known for three very different kinds of writing. What are they?

807. In which Dorothy Sayers' novel does the character Catherine Bendick appear?

808. In which multimedia artform have the following women worked? Yoko Ono, Mary Beth Edelson, Carolee Schneemann, Pauline Oliveros, Meredith Monk, Laurie Anderson, Betsy Damon, Yvonne Rainer, Jill Orr.

642. Golfing greens throughout England were carved with the slogan 'no votes, no golf'.

643. Margaret Abbott, USA, 1904 (it was discontinued after that).

644. Polo.

645. Princess Anne.

646. Her horses won the chariot race.

647. Jacki Joyner-Kersee. Events included in a heptathlon are: 100-metres hurdles, high jump, shot, 200-metres sprint on day one; and on day two, the long jump, javelin and 800 metres.

648. Betty Cuthbert (she won 100m, 200m sprint and relay in 1956; and in 1964 won 400m).

649. Squash.

650. Nine.

651. Evonne Goolagong.

652. The bicycle.

653. Amelia Jenks Bloomer.

654. Elsa Schiaparelli.

655. Rei Kawakubo.

656. Marguerite Duras.

657. Marlene Gorris.

658. Margarethe von Trotta.

659. Leni Riefenstahl.

660. 400m hurdle.

661. Softball.

662. Shane Gould, 1972, 200m, 400m, 200m individual medley in swimming.

663. Dawn Fraser, in 1956, 1960 and 1964 in 100m freestyle.

664. Fatima Whitbread, UK.

665. Javelin.

666. Iuliana Semenova, the Soviet team captain in basketball at 7 feet 1¾ inches tall and 284 lbs.

667. Mexico, Peru and Poland.

668. Ulrike Holmer, a sixteen-year-old West German, who won silver in 1984.

669. Seo Hyang-Soon, seventeen-year-old Korean woman.

670. Twelve in Individual Foil.

671. Marlene Dietrich.

672. They all sang the Blues.

673. Janis Joplin.

674. Lucy Jordan.

675. Janice Robinson – trombone (also leader / composer, 70s)
Willene Barton – alto sax (also leader, 50s)
Carla Bley – keyboards (also sax, 60s)
Vi Redd – alto sax (also soprano sax/ vocals/leader, 60s)
Corky Hale – flute (also harp/ piano/organ/piccolo/cello, 50s)
June Rotenberg – bass, 40s
Dorothy Ashby – harp (also piano/composer, 50s)
Peggy Gilbert – vibes (also reeds/vocals/leader, 20s)
Bridget O'Flynn – drums, 40s
Audrey Hall Petroff – violin (also reeds/piano/leader, 20s)
Sarah McLawler – organ (also piano/vocals, 40s)

Irma Young – ukulele (also alto sax/B-flat soprano sax/ baritone sax/tap dancer, 20s)

Doris Peavey – accordion (also piano/organ, 20s)

Betty Sattley Leeds – tenor sax, 30s

Ann Patterson – reeds (also leader, 70s)

Estelle Slavin – trumpet (also leader, 30s)

676. Xiaoxuan of China.

677. Skating.

678. Canoeing.

679. Nadia Comaneci.

680. Olga Korbut.

681. Meg Christian.

682. *Show Some Emotion*.

683. Laurie Anderson.

684. Robyn Archer.

685. Cards.

686. Gillian Armstrong.

687. Judy Davis.

688. Margaret Fink.

689. Tracy Chapman.

690. *Ariel*. The poem is 'The Applicant' and the book was published in 1966.

691. Marilyn Horne.

692. Joan Sutherland.

693. *Lakmé* and *Madame Butterfly*.

694. *The Lion and the Cobra*.

695. Andrews Sisters.

696. The winners tied, they were

Carrie Steinseifer and Nancy Hogshead, both from the USA.

697. Table tennis.

698. Yachting.

699. Fanny Blankers-Koen.

700. Irina was the daughter of Elizabeta.

701. Joan Benoit in 1984.

702. Anne Audain.

703. Nine in track and field; eleven in swimming.

704. She wore a leg brace as a child and went on to win three gold medals.

705. Valerie Briscoe-Hooks, at Los Angeles 1984.

706. Dawn Fraser.

707. Tessa Sanderson from Britain in 1984.

708. Marathon running.

709. Ingrid Kristiansen from Norway.

710. Althea Gibson.

711. Princess Anne.

712. She doesn't want to get married, and she outwits all the princes who try for her hand.

713. She is a Victorian lady traveller who specializes in great adventures. In *Miss Fanshawe and the Great Dragon Adventure* she sets off to find a dragon, catches it, then releases it to make it happy.

714. Gail Greenough who won the 1986 world showjumping championship.

715. Seventy-year-old, British equestrian Lorna Johnstone.

716. Sappho.

717. Rita Mae Brown in 'Sappho's Reply' in the collection *The Hand That Cradles the Rock*, 1971.

718. *Stoner McTavish* and *Something Shady*.

719. Buying yourself a pair of red shoes / buying yourself a lemon daquiri.

720. Lesbian relationships and all their ups and downs. The title of a novel by Norwegian writer, Gerd Brandenberg.

721. Sappho (Some say nine Muses – but count again. Behold the tenth: Sappho of Lesbos, Plato).

722. They wrote poetry together. An example from one verse is: '. . . shall I stay unwed? That would please me, / for making babies doesn't seem so good, / and it's too anguishing to be a wife.'

723. Louise Labé (1524/25–1566)

724. *The Alice B. Toklas Cook Book*.

725. Grace Slick.

726. Ntozake Shange

727. Elizabeth David.

728. Ursula Pridham.

729. Edna Walling.

730. Sissinghurst.

731. Catherine the Great of Russia.

732. A long, usually silk, dress, sometimes extravagantly orna- mented with lace trimmings and which rustles when the wearer moves, making a sound like frou-frou.

733. Elsa Chauvel.

734. Glen Tomasetti.

735. The Miles Franklin Award.

736. Wendy Harmer.

737. Nancy Reagan in a tribute to Elizabeth Taylor.

738. *Porgy and Bess.*

739. African and Caribbean traditions.

740. Her plaits come up from the hairline to form a ponytail at the crown of her head.

741. Miriam Makeba.

742. A Cappella Choir.

743. Enya.

744. Chrissie Hynde of The Pretenders.

745. Bauhaus.

746. Still life or domestic objects.

747. Edith Somerville and Violet Martin, Irish novelists, cousins and lovers they wrote fourteen works together including *The Real Charlotte* (1894) and *Some Experiences of an Irish RM* (1899).

748. Stage and costume design for *Le coq d'or* (1914), *Les noces* (1923), *The Firebird* (1926).

749. Traditional motifs using batik on silk.

750. They are all Australian artists and are depicted on the

covers of the Penguin Australian Women's Library.

751. Guerrilla Girls

752. Ola Cohn.

753. Haiku.

754. *Post Partum Document.*

755. Dora, Harriet, Harriet, Marianne, Amy, Mina, Sylvia, Hilda, Dorothy.

756. Dorothy Richardson.

757. Katherine Philips.

758. Carolina Nairne (1766–1845)

759. *Sense and Sensibility.*

760. Marie de Sévigné.

761. Music – she was a concert pianist and composer.

762. Elizabeth Maconchy.

763. Edith Sitwell.

764. Béatrice de Die, Countess of Die.

765. Old wine flagons.

766. They were Australian pastoralists who made a great success of establishing themselves as partners, in spite of social pressures against them.

767. *The Family at Misrule / Little Mother Meg.*

768. *Dert and Do.*

769. She's a woman.

770. *The Traffic in Women.*

771. Jane Austen in *Persuasion.*

772. Ironing (the story is called 'I Stand Here Ironing', 1954).

773. Katharine Hepburn.

774. Katharine Hepburn.

775. Walt Disney (amongst the things she wrote is, 'Who's Afraid of the Big Bad Wolf?').

776. Amy Johnson, aviatrix (1903–1941).

777. Grace Paley (b. 1922).

778. [Nellie] Harper Lee.

779. *Don't Fall Off the Mountain.*

780. Marilyn Monroe.

781. She is the youngest grandmaster in the history of chess.

782. Judy Grahn, 1974 in the long poem *A Woman Is Talking to Death.*

783. Robin Morgan in *Monster*, 1972.

784. Alice Walker (In search of my mother's garden I found my own, 1974).

785. *The House of All Nations*, 1938.

786. Dorothy Parker.

787. Helen Reddy.

788. Jeannie Lewis

789. The flute.

790. Ferron.

791. Opera.

792. Mozart.

793. Clarinet.

794. Gertrude Stein.

795. Painting.

796. Robyn Kahukiwa did the paintings and drawings, Patricia Grace wrote the text.

797. Celie.

798. *The Paradise Papers.*

799. *A Woman's Guide to Domestic Insanity.*

800. Jane Campion.

801. *The Australian Women's Book Review.*

802. The Australian Feminist Book Fortnight.

803. *Belles Lettres* and *The Women's Review of Books.*

804. Catherine.

805. *Villette.*

806. Detective fiction, religious writing and translations of Dantë.

807. *Gaudy Night.*

808. Performance art.

Sources

Achterberg, Jeanne. 1990. *Woman as Healer*. London: Rider Books.

Alic, Margaret. 1986. *Hypatia's Heritage: A History of Women in Science from Antiquity to the Late Nineteenth Century*. London: The Women's Press.

Barnstone, Aliki and Barnstone, Willis. (Eds). 1987. *A Book of Women Poets from Antiquity to Now*. New York: Schocken Books.

Blonski, Annette, Creed, Barbara and Freda Freiberg. (Eds.). 1987. *Don't Shoot Darling: Women's Independent Filmmaking in Australia*. Melbourne: Greenhouse.

Blue, Adrianne. 1988. *Faster, Higher, Further: Women's Triumphs and Disasters at the Olympics*. London: Virago Press.

Burke, Janine. 1980. *Australian Women Artists, 1840–1940*. Melbourne: Greenhouse.

Chadwick, Whitney. 1985. *Women Artists and the Surrealist Movement*. London: Thames & Hudson.

Chadwick, Whitney. 1990. *Women, Art and Society*. London: Thames & Hudson.

Gimbutas, Marija. 1990. *The Language of the Goddess*. London: Thames & Hudson.

Hart, George. 1986. *A Dictionary of Egyptian Gods and Goddesses*. London, Boston and Henley: Routledge & Kegan Paul.

Henry, Sondra and Emily Taitz. 1990. *Written Out of History: Our Jewish Foremothers*. New York: Biblio Press.

Jezic, Diane Peacock. 1988. *Women Composers: The Lost Tradition*. New York: The Feminist Press.

Lanker, Brian, with a Foreword by Maya Angelou. 1989. *I Dream a World: Portraits of Black Women Who Changed America*. New York: Stewart, Tabori & Chang.

Loewenberg, Bert James and Ruth Bogin. (Eds.) 1976. *Black Women in Nineteenth-Century American Life*. University Park and London: Penn State University Press.

Morgan, Robin. (Ed.) 1984. *Sisterhood is Global*. New York: Penguin Books.

Murphy, Kate. 1990. *Firsts: The Livewire Book of British Women Achievers*. London: The Women's Press.

Neuls-Bates, Carol. (Ed.) 1982. *Women in Music: An Anthology of Source Readings from the Middle Ages to the Present*. New York: Harper & Row.

Ogilvie, Marilyn Bailey. 1986. *Women in Science: Antiquity through the Nineteenth Century*. Cambridge, MA: MIT Press.

Partnow, Elaine. 1986 *The Quotable Woman: From Eve to 1799*. New York, and Bicester, England: Facts on File Publications.

Partnow, Elaine. 1982. *The Quotable Woman: 1800–1981*. New York and Bicester: Facts on File Publications.

Placksin, Sally. 1982. *Jazz Women: 1900 to the Present, Their Words, Lives and Music*. London and Sydney: Pluto Press.

Petersen, Karen and J.J. Wilson. 1976/1985. *Women Artists: Recognition and Reappraisal from the Early Middle Ages to the Twentieth Century*. New York: Harper & Row; London: The Women's Press.

Radi, Heather. (Ed.) 1988. *200 Australian Women: A Redress Anthology*. Sydney: Women's Redress Press Inc.

Roth, Moira. (Ed.) 1983. *The Amazing Decade: Women and Performance Art in America, 1970–1980*. Los Angeles: Astro Artz.

Scutt, Jocelynne A. 1991. *Women and the Law*. Sydney: The Law Book Company.

Seager, Joni and Ann Olson. 1986. *Women in the World: An International Atlas.* London and Sydney: Pan Books.

Sertima, Ivan Van. (Ed.) 1989. *Black Women in Antiquity.* New Brunswick and London: Transaction Books.

Spender, Dale. 1983. *Women of Ideas (And What Men Have Done To Them).* London: Paandora Press.

Spender, Dale. (Ed.) 1983. *Feminist Theorists. Three Centuries of Women's Intellectual Traditions.* London: The Women's Press.

Stanley, Autumn. 1992. 'Once and Future Power: Women as Inventors'. *Women's Studies International Forum.* Vol. 15, No. 2.

Sullivan, Constance. 1990. *Women Photographers,* with an essay by Eugenia Parry Janis. London: Virago.

Sulter, Maud. (Ed.) 1990. *Passion: Discourses on Blackwomen's Creativity.* Photography by Ingrid Pollard. Hebden Bridge, Yorkshire: Urban Fox Press.

Tanner, Leslie B. (Ed.) 1970. *Voices from Women's Liberation.* New Jersey: NAL.

Troemel-Ploetz, Senta. 1990. 'Mileva Einstein-Marić: the woman who did Einstein's mathematics'. *Women's Studies International Forum.* Vol. 13, No. 5.

Tufts, Eleanor. 1974. *Our Hidden Heritage: Five Centuries of Women Artists.* New York and London: Paddington Press.

Uglow, Jennifer S. (Ed.) *1982. The Macmillan Dictionary of Women's Biography.* London: Macmillan.

Waithe, Mary Ellen. (Ed). 1989. *A History of Women Philosophers, Vol. 2 / 500–1600.* Dordrecht, Boston and London: Kluwer Academic Publishers.

Walker, Barbara G. 1983. *The Woman's Book of Myths and Secrets.* San Francisco: Harper & Row.

WIFT. 1991. *Women Working in Film, Television and Video.* Sydney: Women in Film and Television Inc.

Index

Grace, Patricia 212, 796
graffiti 582, 603, 629, 633
Graham, Bette 59
Grahn, Judy 782
Grapefruit 263, 605
'Grass' 441
Grass is Singing, The 442
Gray Panthers 609
Greece: Ancient 373
Greenaway, Kate 751
Greene, Catherine 61
Greenough, Gail 714
Greer, Germaine 531
Grenville, Kate 144
Grey, Lady Jane 386
Grimké, Sarah Moore 608
Groen, Alma de 734
Groover, Jan 746
Grosz, Elizabeth 617
Group, The 187
Guerrilla Girls 751
Guggenheim, Peggy 795
Gunn, Aeneas 451

H. D. *see* Doolittle, Hilda (H. D.)
Hades 413
Hadewych/Hadewijch of Antwerp 95, 314
hair 635
Hale, Corky 675
Hall Petroff, Audrey 675
Hall, Radclyffe 293, 300, 301
Hammer of Witches, The 140
Hand that Cradles the Rock, The 717
Hanff, Helene 422
Hanging Rock 447, 497
Hansberry, Lorraine 206
Hanscombe, Gillian 306
Hardisty, Sue 208
Hari, Mata 573
Harity 373
Harmer, Wendy 736
Harper Lee, Nellie 778
Harris, La-Neeta 595
Hatshepsut 171, 220, 374, 406
Hawaii 373
Haworth 487
Head, Bessie 418, 593

Heagney, Muriel 560
health and healing 9, 20, 28, 32, 33, 38, 40, 41, 89, 97, 101, 308, 541, *see also* medicine
Hearing Trumpet, The 460
Hebe-Hera-Hecate 49
Hecate Trivia 613
Hecate's Charms 306
Helen 7
Héloïse 587
Hepburn, Katharine 773, 774
Heptameron, The 175
Hepworth, Barbara 751, 763
Hera 113
Herean Games 113
Heremakhonon 310
Herland 390
Herland (NSW) 391
Herschel, Caroline 2, 22, 74
Hesse, Eva 751
Hewett, Dorothy 637
hieroglyphs 118
High Tide 686
Hildegard of Bingen 20, 95, 411, 483
Hiroshima, mon amour 656
Ho, Lady 377
Hogarth Press 339
Hogshead, Nancy 696
Holland *see* Netherlands (Holland)
Hollander, Nicole 350
Holliday, Billie 672
Holmer, Ulrike 668
Holtby, Winifred 294
Hong Kingston, Maxine 418
Honnamma 515
Horae 49
Horne, Marilyn 691
Horta, Maria Teresa 315
House of All Nations, The 785
housewives and housework 557
How to Observe 580
Hrotsvita of

Gandersheim 202
Huang O 491
Hudgins, Margaret 543
Huggins, Erica 543
Hulme, Keri 332
humourists and humour 98, 349, 350, 514, 602, 629, 633, 719, 736, 774, 786
Hunter, Ruby 494
Hurston, Zora Neale 258
Hyang-Soon, Seo 669
Hygeia 28
hygiene 26
'Hymn to Her' 744
Hymne à l'amour 264
Hynde, Chrissie 744
Hypatia 216
hysteria 37

Ibu people 132
Iceland 178, 469
'Ich bin von Kopf' 671
Ifuru 371
immolation 526
immunization 34
'In search of my mother's garden' 784
in vitro fertilization 623, 624, 625
Inanna 28
incest 248
income 431
India 373, 432, 471, 473, 475, 526; rape law 524
indigenous people 212, 214, 332, 336, 338, 370, 464, 465, 477, 521, 796, *see also* Australian Aborigines
Indonesia 128
industrial relations 150, 560, 641; equal rights 560, 641; theorists 240, 282; trade unions 97, 273, 560; women's strikes 156, 178, 179; world union 240, *see also* work
infibulation 525
Ingleton, Sue 799
innoculation 35, 36
Inquisition 571

SPINIFEX PRESS

is an independent publishing venture that
publishes innovative and controversial feminist
titles by Australian and international authors.
Our list includes fiction, poetry and non-fiction
across a diverse range of topics with a radical and
optimistic feminist perspective.

*Spinifex Press was awarded the international
Pandora New Venture Award for 1991 from
Women in Publishing (UK).*

OTHER BOOKS AVAILABLE FROM SPINIFEX PRESS

The Falling Woman
Susan Hawthorne

Top Twenty Title, New Zealand Women's Book Festival, 1992

The Falling Woman memorably dramatises a desert journey in which two women confront ancient and modern myths, ranging from the Garden of Eden to the mystique of epilepsy, and the mysteries of the universe itself. In the guise of three personae – Stella, Estella, Estelle – the falling woman struggles to find the map for her life and meet the challenge of her own survival.

'A remarkable, lyrical first novel that weaves together such disparate themes as the mystery of epilepsy, love between women, and an odyssey across the Australian desert.'   – *Ms Magazine.*

'Hawthorne shows assurance, a powerful historical and cultural imagination and a rich feel for language.'   – John Hanrahan, *Age.*

'This is a beautiful book, written with powerful insight and captivating originality.'   – Julia Hancock, *LOTL.*

Angels of Power
and other reproductive creations
edited by Susan Hawthorne and Renate Klein

1991 Australian Feminist Fortnight Favourite

In the tradition of Mary Shelley's *Frankenstein*, the writers in this book use technological developments as their starting point in tracing the consequences of reproductive technologies. Imagination, vision and humour come together and demonstrate that women can resist the power of godlike scientists who long to create monsters and angels. With contributions by writers from Australia, New Zealand, Canada and USA.

'*Angels of Power* is an important ground-breaking anthology ...'
— Karen Lamb, *Age*.

'*Angels of Power* should head the reading list of any course in ethics and reproductive technology.'
— Karin Lines, *Editions*.

'... renders ethical issues imaginatively through fiction and contributes significantly to this important debate.'
— Irina Dunn, *Sydney Morning Herald*.

Sybil:
The Glide of Her Tongue
Gillian Hanscombe

'Gillian Hanscombe performs a feat of lesbian imagination in this stunning sequence. Her sybilic voice, familiar and strange at once, radiates both vision and anger in a prose that echoes the music of our thoughts back to us. *Sybil* gives us a lesbian erotic, a lesbian politics, a lesbian tradition, grounded in what Suniti Namjoshi defines as the prophetic. Welcome to lesbian imagination singing at full range.'

– Daphne Marlatt

'That *Sybil* happily bears comparison with the works of Sappho, Virginia Woolf and Adrienne Rich is, in my view, a measure of just how important this work is to lesbian literature, and therefore to literature in general.'

– Suniti Namjoshi

'*Sybil: The Glide of Her Tongue* is a prophetic fugue in lesbian past, present and future time, Sybilline tidings of lesbian existence.'

– Mary Meigs

'O I am enamoured of *Sybil*. Gillian Hanscombe is one of the most insightfully ironic, deliciously lyrical voices we have writing amongst us today.'

– Betsy Warland

'A book where the lesbian voice meditates the essential vitality of she dykes who have visions. A book where Gillian Hanscombe's poetry opens up meaning in such a way that it provides for beauty and awareness, for a space where one says yes to a lesbian we of awareness.'

– Nicole Brossard

'*Sybil* is an exciting and compelling work. It is hard to think of any poet in Australia who can equal Hanscombe's virtuosity and power.'

– Bev Roberts, *Australian Book Review*

If Passion Were a Flower
Lariane Fonseca

'Here the shadows of the plants were miraculously distinct. She noticed the separate grains of earth in the flower beds as if she had a micro-scope stuck to her eye. She saw the intricacy of the twigs of every tree. Each blade of grass was distinct and the markings of the veins and petals.'

– Virginia Woolf, *Orlando.*

Bombay-born photographer, Lariane Fonseca was inspired by the writing of Virginia Woolf and the paintings of Georgia O'Keefe. In this breathtaking book she displays not only expertise but a sensitivity to the visual beauty of the world around her. These photographs allow us to glimpse the intricate wonder of nature.

'If you appreciate great coffee table art buy the book … it's a bargain.'
– Rosie Cox, *Melbourne Star Observer.*

Too Rich

Melissa Chan

'You can never be too thin or too rich,' said Wallis Simpson, Duchess of Windsor. But Francesca Miles, independent feminist detective, disagrees. When one of the richest men in Sydney is found dead in his penthouse she teams up with Inspector Joe Barnaby in a mystery that follows the trials and tribulations of a family that should have everything money can buy.

'... an intelligent and politically interesting plot.'

– Venetia Brissenden,
Mean Streets.

'Hooray for Melissa Chan and may she write many more whodunnits.'

– *WEL-Informed.*

'... an immensely entertaining read.'

– *Ita.*

'One of the best Australian whodunnits to surface recently – the characterisation is superb, the style elegant, and there are manifold lightly ironic touches.'

– Ray Davie, *Age.*

Getting Your Man
Melissa Chan

Getting your man, getting the right man, is not always easy. But women, whether they be piece-workers, housewives, artists, business women or farmers, know just how to get their man.

In the tradition of Thelma and Louise, Melissa Chan's second book is a collection of humorous short stories that revolve around the theme of women's revenge.

'This is romance with a feminist message and a crime twist ... just right for reading on the beach in between catching a few waves.'
— Renata Sirger, *Sisters in Crime*.